Butterflies, Zebras, Moonbeams

Butterflies, Zebras, Moonbeams

Ceilidh Michelle

Palimpsest Press
1171 Eastlawn Ave.
Windsor, Ontario. N8S 3J1
www.palimpsestpress.ca

Printed and bound in Canada.
Cover design and book typography by Ellie Hastings.
Edited by Ginger Pharand.

Palimpsest Press would like to thank the Canada Council for
the Arts and the Ontario Arts Council for their support of our
publishing program. We also acknowledge the assistance of the
Government of Ontario through the Ontario Book Publishing
Tax Credit.

LIBRARY AND ARCHIVES CANADA CATALOGUING IN PUBLICATION

TITLE: Butterflies, zebras, moonbeams / Ceilidh Michelle.
NAMES: Michelle, Ceilidh, 1987- author.
IDENTIFIERS: Canadiana (print) 20190140011
              Canadiana (ebook) 2019014002X

ISBN 9781989287309 (SOFTCOVER) | ISBN 9781989287316 (EPUB)
ISBN 9781989287323 (KINDLE) | ISBN 9781989287330 (PDF)

CLASSIFICATION: LCC PS8626.I275 B88 2019 | DDC C813/.6—DC23

*This book is dedicated to the memory of
Nathan Wilson.*

Well, she's walking through the clouds
With a circus mind that's running wild,
Butterflies and Zebras
And Moonbeams and fairytales.
That's all she ever thinks about.
Riding with the wind.

When I'm sad, she comes to me,
With a thousand smiles she gives to me free.
It's alright, she says it's alright,
Take anything you want from me,
Anything.
Fly on little wing.

– Jimi Hendrix

and fairytales

Nothing was ever as glamorous or smooth as it sounded. The days were rough and we were rough in them. We were disgruntled and lost, lonely and insecure. We ate too much or not enough, we woke up ugly, we behaved badly. Transient was too kind a word, it was more like the chaos of a mosh pit, which the Quebecois kids called "thrashing." Only when they said it, it sounded like "trashing." This worked because it felt that way—we wound up scattered on the streets of the morning like pieces of trash.

I'm speaking for no one. I'm speaking for people I used to know. I want to tell the stories of my friends before they're forgotten in the hustle of growing old. But then you don't need to know my motives. You're as full of time bombs and unforeseen disaster as I am.

I still feel the gruelling crusade of being twenty-something, but now on the other side, I feel it in physical after-affects, the way anxiety kicks in only after the danger has faded. Sabotage was a word I knew and loved. It met me on the streets at night. It called me crazy. But crazy set me apart. It made me real.

I scribbled my own raggedy lyrics like *Don't be a coward* on the covers of my drugstore notebooks because it was meant to convey cryptic profundity. I used to fall for lead singers and frontmen. Then I liked guitar players. That meant I was more mature and had better taste. I wore outfits strategically, wanting to catch the eye of the world. I wanted people to ask me about my wisdom. I could convert somebody.

If I'd stayed behind in my maritime town, I would have been stuck as a nurse or a teacher or a teen mother. I went to Montreal instead. In Montreal, I could get a four-dollar beer from a dépanneur. I climbed rickety staircases and went spelunking down graffitied alleyways, combed through record stores smelling of mildewed cardboard. There was room for everyone at the record store: academic jazz virtuosos, clowns, stars, surf, punk, poets…all you had to do was find the right shoe-size, the sound that fit your feet to dance, to rock, to lose your mind or make it up.

Joanna Love

Standing on the corner, suitcase in my hand. Some woman on a bike had just been hit by a car and a crowd had gathered on Guy and Maisonneuve, mostly people standing around. I stood there too, eating an orange with fingers stiff from the cold and wondering what would happen next when a boy waved at me from across the street. I glanced over my shoulder because I knew no one but there was nobody behind me. I waved back slowly, as if under the sea.

He wore purple bell-bottoms and a velvet jacket, his afro like a storm cloud. He came across the street urgently, like I was late to our meeting. When he reached my side, he offered up a silver flask and said his name was Jude.

We talked mildly about the scene on the street. The taxi had fled and the woman sat on the lip of the road with her face in her hands, yelling and smoking, her bike crumpled beside her in the gutter.

"That happens all the time here," Jude told me.

"What else happens here? I've only been in the city a week."

"Why's that?"

"Because last week was when I arrived."

"No," he said, and jerked his chin toward a side street,

indicating that we should head in its direction. "Why are you here?"

I took a swig of the silver flask and let it burn along my tongue a while before swallowing. The day, already old and overcast, grew darker as we walked along to a rhythm of sirens and honking horns. The cacophony of cursing Frenchmen and jabbering families was as significant as wallpaper because I didn't yet know the words.

"I came to make music and write songs," I said.

"Oh, you're a musician." Jude pointed to his apartment, a stone building with fire escapes hanging off it like dirty laundry, the front steps cracked down the middle as if they'd been smitten by god.

"Not yet," I said. "But soon."

Jude had a yellow bedroom at the top of the stairs. The room had nothing in it except a mattress and a record player. He had five identical cardigan sweaters in the closet. We sat up all night playing records and smoking pot and Jude told me about all the drugs he'd ever done in his life and the different ways they affected his guitar tone. He talked about his band, The Crying Dads. We might have taken something to stay up all night, but I don't remember now. I only remember the way he talked about composition as if it was beyond everyone else's understanding but his own.

I told him about my songs, or my ideas for songs, how I could play four chords on an acoustic guitar but wanted to do everything else. I'd heard of an instrument called a theremin, which was really just an instrument for playing the air. Jude's ideas were in theory and mathematics.

I fell asleep on his bare mattress in the grey seediness of dawn. Jude laid out on the hardwood floor, his hands on his chest like a mummified king. Scowling in his sleep. His hair made a fine enough pillow. When I woke up, mid-morning sun made me squint. My face was pressed against a Grace

Jones record, her face square and bold as a skyscraper. The yellow bedroom full of light, the record player crackling like an old fire.

The Crying Dads jammed in a place near the river, behind the hockey arena. The building used to house Ukrainian immigrants after the war, but now it belonged to the musicians. The lobby was dark and full of mirrors, the carpets filthy. Fake potted ferns protruded from the corners, ratty with cobwebs.

I followed Jude up a flight of stairs, then down a flight, then up another one, around a corner, into a narrow hall under scintillating florescent lights. Unmarked doorways punctuated the walls, each one a lid over screams of weird guitar, smashing violent drums, sometimes a hollering man. The sharp smell of mildewed carpet.

Finally, Jude stopped, went back a few doors. "I always forget which space it is." He knocked loudly. I shifted from foot to foot. The florescent light winked above our heads, the colour of veins. He'd barely spoken since we'd met up that evening but maybe it was just his way. "Come on," he hollered, knocking again with an angry fist.

There was a sudden crash from within and a fat freckled kid materialized, grinning and squinting like a stoned cat. "Sorry man. I thought the knocking was in my head." Jude stalked past him into the space.

"My name's B." I stuck out my hand to shake.

He turned his vacant glance on me. "I'm Polka Dot," he said, shyly ducking his head. "I play the drums."

I followed him inside, got a whiff of the room, and began breathing through my mouth. A brown couch had been heaved crookedly into the corner. A Pearl drum set, nice in theory but fucked up in reality, sat half-destroyed at the back, pockmarked guitars propped up beside it.

The walls and ceiling, painted black, gave the windowless room a claustrophobic feeling, like being inside a mouth. There were lamps on the floor, here and there, with mottled ceramic bases and cracked, bulb-burned lampshades. The light made everything seem melted. The carpet was covered in indescribable detritus, potato chips ground into the pile with scattered guitar picks, broken strings.

Over the couch hung a tied-dyed head-shop tapestry with a cheap rendering of Bob Marley's face. Strung along the ceiling were seven teddy bears and grotesque dolls, ratty like they'd been found in a gutter, bloated with puddle water and cigarette smoke.

Polka Dot flopped down on the couch, rediscovered a muddy bong, and gazed off into space, drumming his fingers.

Jude glared at him. "Where the hell is everyone? We said jam at seven, correct?"

The kid startled. "Yeah, that's right. Guess they're running late."

"Clearly." Jude rolled his eyes at me, as if I shared the burden of his impatience.

I went and sat by Polka Dot. I'd brought a notebook with me and started messing around in it. It was a great place to hide when I ran out of things to say.

After a few minutes of Jude tensely tuning his guitar, the jam space door crashed open and two boys, presumably the late members of the Crying Dads, began trying to shove their way into the dark room simultaneously. A violent wrestling match ensued and was only broken up by Jude smashing his fist into the one of the drum cymbals. The boys removed themselves from the carpet abashedly—one of them came over to Polka Dot and gave him a high-five.

"Fuck the metro, am I right?" he said. A skinny Japanese kid in a striped sweater, he tried to bestow a high-five on Jude as well, but Jude pointedly crossed his arms across his chest and eyed the kid with disdain. The kid ran his hand through his hair as if he'd meant it to be that way. "Actually, it was A Minor's fault," and he nodded over at the long-haired boy he'd been wrestling with moments before. "He tried to hop the metro and got busted. Fine, whatever. But what does he tell the cops his name is? John Smith. John fucking Smith." He stopped talking when he noticed Jude coming toward him. "Sorry, sorry, sorry. Fuck the metro." And then he called over at me. "Hi. My name's Bamboo." He began fiddling around with a plastic keyboard, attached somehow to a Flying V guitar. "Are you our first groupie?"

"Depends on how good your music is," I said.

"I can see you've met the Pasta Rasta," the kid named A Minor said to me.

"Who?"

"Jude has an Italian mother who makes an incredible sauce." A Minor waggled his eyebrows. "And his father is of the Caribbean persuasion? Isn't that right Jude?"

Jude threw a drumstick at him. "A Minor's permafried. Tell her about the time you drank the mescaline and saw spiders." But A Minor busied himself with changing a string on his bass.

"How'd you all meet?" I asked.

"We worked in the kitchen of a steakhouse down-town," A Minor said. "When I met Jude he always wore this trench coat and only drank tonic water. I thought he must be a serial killer. But then I found out he was just a musician."

Jude led their jams like a football coach, a sundog guitar slung around his skinny waist. Shouting key changes and song names, telling them when to slow down or speed up, directing and instructing. He captained a set that had sweet spots of melody and dazzling noise. Jude shredded subtle dots of sound, picking and swerving around bass lines played by the boy called A Minor, who sang in a voice that sounded like it came from all around him.

I went to every one of their jams after that. When I heard them play, I got the urge to run home and pick up my own guitar. But I knew it wouldn't sound the same. After band rehearsals, we headed up the road to a little basement bar and crowded around a table in the corner. We weren't the only musicians there. The bartender was in a band, the barmaids were in bands, whoever cleaned the toilets was probably in a band.

Bamboo told me the ideas he had for his Casio keyboards. He wanted to turn his guitars into a massive synth, a big cyborg of sound. He waved his fingers frantically. He spilled his beer twice. While he spoke, I saw Jude watching me the whole time, noticed the sharp sparks of his eyes.

Polka Dot, A Minor, and Bamboo left in a blur, the shadows of the loamy cave bar reeling. They went off stumbling into the night, arms over each other's shoulders, singing *Atlantic City* and crying the crocodile tears of a blackout drunk. Jude sank lower in his chair, leaving little piles of pennies and crumpled receipts in his wake.

The sky was coming back to life when we finally hit the street. Through the empty morning of Montreal, up into the narrow cobbled one-way streets of the Plateau with alleyways you could look down forever, hanging fire-escapes, turrets and looming windows, little shops for incense and djembes and smoked meat sandwiches. Our voices came out in shaky reverberations, bouncing against the building faces, up into the back-and-white sky.

shut up and play yer guitar

Jude and I were going to make music. He came to my apartment in the evening, carrying a guitar case and a tambourine. I had a tiny place with tiles on the floor—Jude said it reminded him of a hospital. His forehead beaded with sweat from climbing the four flights, he stood there looking around the room as if he'd wound up there by accident.

"You want a beer or something?" I asked him, hovering.

"No. Thanks." He pulled his flask from his back pocket and flung himself down on the red couch I had dragged up from the street. "Let's get to it. We'll put together a set list of five or six songs that you can play live. There's your first demo."

I wanted to kick him back out so I could think things over. Instead, I picked up my acoustic guitar which banged a hollow knock on my knee. Conscious of how much space his legs took up when I sat beside him, I went through tunes I had penned since coming to the city, open chord jams about the usual junk.

"Okay," Jude finally said, running his long fingers through his hair. "I see what you're trying to do." Trying to do because I guess I wasn't doing it yet. He unbuckled his guitar case and brought out his own instrument. "We

19

gotta fill out the bones." He began noodling complex riffs, fingers blurring along the strings. Showing me what I could do if I got in ten thousand hours. "...you know, it's like the Mahavishnu Orchestra. North American sounds are so limited by pop culture. I want to record the vibration of the earth, or go to India and learn new scales. Forget the North American formula." He was talking about my formula. I wanted to add something to the conversation but it wasn't a conversation.

We broke down my songs like we were performing an autopsy, exposing the spindly tendons of notes. He took my songs from pencil sketches to sculptures. I wanted to preserve the sounds he made, bottle them in glass jars so I could study them when I was by myself. But when I tried to follow him he said, "No, no, stop."

"What?" I lit a cigarette and stuck it in the strings of my guitar like I'd seen Bob Dylan do. Jude rolled his eyes at me when I did that.

"Try that verse again, only add this," and he played something impossible. "You hear that, how the notes go into the Aeolian mode and then resolve?"

I said, "No. I don't hear that. I don't even know what that is."

Sometimes Jude brought me over records that he'd dredged up from the bottom of the vinyl sea. He spent hours digging through milk crates. "Anything you want, anything good, you have to spend hours doing," he instructed didactically, pacing the floors and punctuating the air with his big hands. "You want good records? You gotta hunt them out. You want to play music? You gotta pick up your guitar." His favourite thing to ask me was, "What is the foundation to any practice?" as if he were my coach and I was the boxer fucked up in the corner of the ring. "Discipline," I would answer in sarcastic monotone. But no answer would have pleased him—it was that displeasure that kept him searching for better sounds.

"Lightnin' Hopkins!" he yelled one time, bursting into my living room. I sat on the windowsill beside a stack of Salvation Army paperback books, practicing scales and letting the spring night blow clean air into my apartment. He held up a record half-falling out of a split cardboard sleeve. *Lightnin' Strikes* had a photo of an old man with a cigarette in his mouth, sunglasses, mean-mugging. "People are fools for overlooking this gem." We were all fools to Jude. Inside his ears were tiny gold gears and screws, turning, clicking, whizzing like an infinite pocket watch. He snapped his fingers everywhere we went. He heard music in the street, coming up from the sidewalk.

He played in four other bands besides the Crying Dads: an acid jazz group with ten university students, a reggae funk band with musicians twice his age, a progressive-rock band that prided themselves on their ability to execute unexpected time signatures, and then, after I'd been playing guitar for about a year or so, he played with me.

Every once in a while you could go down into one of those anonymous jazz clubs with plastic curtains over the door to keep out the cold and you could find Jude onstage with some combo. Hunched over a heavy Les Paul, behind a big fat vocalist whose voice was like the claws of God scratching across your heart. The way Jude played crawled over your flesh—it went into your follicles and made your hairs rise up in an exultant dance. It was crazy. When he played like that, it was easy to forgive his moods and attitudes. He was an obedient vessel, a good little channel. He put in the hours so that the sound emptied itself out of him completely, instead of halfway and half-assed.

Jude told me that he'd grown up in Winnipeg raised by his mother, who was white. He'd never met his father. All the kids at school called him Nigger and Paki. Like grease splashing from a frying pan, they were words that would scald you if they splattered too close, leaving hard little scars.

He moved to Toronto and tried to play in the clubs. But the old men were purists and never let him get onstage. He wound up homeless. He slept on rooftops and in an empty vending machine he found in the alley. He came to Montreal for the same reasons as me. Trying to escape the little hatreds of little people.

Lovage

The bar where I played my first gig, full of pool tables and slot machines, was close enough to my apartment that if I made a fool of myself I could beat a hasty retreat back home. I had to wait until the hockey game ended before I could play. I sat there clenching the neck of my guitar, hoping the Habs would win. The old men in jerseys bellowed at the television screen, slamming down their beer mugs, eyeing each other tensely in case someone was disloyal. They'd tear me apart if I tried to follow a losing hockey game with a couple of stupid songs.

Jude said he'd play with me but he showed up late, distractedly pulling up a chair and grumbling about how he was doing me a favour. That I really shouldn't be playing in public yet. "I don't think we'll make money off this show," he added. "It's probably a waste of time."

I eyed the doorman. He swore and threw peanuts at the television, tore at his hair. People came and went through the door. Nothing existed off the ice. Jude was right—we'd walk out of here as broke as the day we were born. I went outside to have a cigarette.

"We should have practiced this weekend," he shouted after me.

As if there'd been time. Jude had shown up at my apartment uninvited, with Polka Dot and Bamboo and a case of beer. They played a deadly game of Monopoly in which no one won and the board was tossed across the room three times. I found Jude on Sunday morning, curled up on my couch cradling an unopened bottle of wine.

That first gig was about as brutal as gigs can go. I felt like I was standing on the ledge of a tall building wanting to jump but unable to make up my mind. Why the hell did anybody ever get onstage?

The Habs won the game but there had been shootout after shootout, death matches, power plays, or whatever the hell they did to drag the game out for an extra hour. When we finally got onstage, the crowd was emotionally exhausted, their eyes suspicious as we set up our gear. The sound-man was wasted and slumped in the booth, his head lolling.

People vaguely nodded to the thin sound of my playing but I couldn't hear a thing—it was a mangled mess of noise. After two songs Jude took over and buried everything in layers of shredding guitar. I tried to keep up by playing the same three chords over and over but he yelled, "B, that's enough," in front of everyone. He broke into *Shine on You Crazy Diamond*. Drunk people swayed back and forth, sloshing beer and shouting, "*Free Bird!*" I put down my guitar and sat on the aluminum folding chair with my hands in my lap and no one even noticed.

"I wanna believe you work on these songs when we all go home, but from the sounds of it all you do is jerk off." Jude paced back and forth, his guitar forgotten on the floor.

"I can't help it, I have an addiction," Bamboo protested.

"I told you I wanted to work on those polyrhythms," Jude said.

A Minor said, "Polly? Check out Polly ova here," in a mafioso accent.

"Fuck Polly and his rhythms," added Polka Dot from behind the drum kit.

Jude threw his cigarette to the floor. "This is band rehearsal not amateur hour. Jesus fucking Christ. You know what's happening at the next gig. If we don't make a success of it, it's gonna ruin us. " I subtly ground out the smoking carpet. Their jam space was going to burn to the ground, either from Jude's cigarettes or his anger.

We had been sitting here for three hours listening to his tirades. The band would get a few minutes into a song and Jude would freak out all again. He was like a dog that could hear frequencies we couldn't. He said, "I'm taking five. When I get back, so help me God you jokers had better have improved your material." And he stormed out of the room, slamming the door three times in a row.

"I must be a masochist," Polka Dot said as soon as the room fell into peace.

A Minor agreed. "It's not a band, it's a dictatorship."

"Let's save the deductions for when we're over a drink, shall we?" Bamboo told him. He was wearing a racoon hat that looked like it'd been chewed on.

"Fine." A Minor rummaged around behind the couch and came up with a six pack. Cracking a beer, he said, "Now where was I?"

"What did Jude mean about the next gig?" I asked. The smells of the room went away once you'd been there for an hour or so. I felt like I'd been in their jam space for days.

The boys exchanged glances. "The next gig is with our nemesis," A Minor said.

"Your nemesis?"

Polka Dot pattered on the drums and Bamboo began fluttering out a creepy radio-drama organ sound on the keyboard to set the mood.

"Our nemesis is a band called Milky Pete and the Mammograms," said Bamboo. He stood in the middle of the room and spread his hands as if setting the stage, trying to get me to envision his story. "Milky Pete and the Mammograms are from Toronto, but they came here for the cheap rent. Their merch table is like an outlet mall. They don't just have band shirts, they have an entire branded wardrobe. They use the word *branding* all the time. We played with them last month, and Polka Dot fell off his stool and knocked over his drum kit."

"That's not how it happened," Polka Dot shouted.

Bamboo ignored him. "Anyway, there was a bunch of things that went sideways on us. Now Jude says we have to show them up."

"We should get them hooked on hard drugs and ruin their lives," said A Minor.

"I'll be right back." I wandered out into the hallway to find Jude. He'd promised me that we'd go over some of my tunes after the Crying Dads jam tonight but I thought the timing might be bad.

I also wondered what, if anything, I was capable of accomplishing as a lone woman in an atmosphere full of strategizing, schmoozing men. Did anyone care what I had to offer? Did I care? I stood still in the hallway and my thoughts detached me from the linearity of my life.

At the end of the hall I could see the open fire escape door, Jude's silhouette slouching against the black lace of tree branches. The pigeons huddled around him, commiserating. It sounded like they were saying, "Poor Jude, poor Jude," over and over.

We Only Come Out at Night

Nighttime jams muddied with the grit of overdrive pedals, fuzzed out vocals, neon slot machines. Late night venues frequented by drunken young people with kitchen haircuts, curious and hopeful, on the watch for something inspiring enough to compel them to run home and sculpt a response. Bands were born on the sidewalk outside. For some reason, homeless people always chose to close in on these kids—of all people to ask change from. Every band was broke as hell from guest-listing their broke-as-hell friends.

The places to play in Montreal seemed to change owners all the time, DIY venues busted by cops or shut down over noise complaints. Sometimes the owner of an after-hours spot would get accused of assaulting a girl and then he'd have to skip town. We weren't safe, but the community tried to weed out its predators.

Some venues had been abandoned to the city, buried beneath CAUTION tape and graffiti, posters from concerts long past still taped to the window. No one really got paid to play. You'd write $5 on a piece of paper and hoped people had money at the door. You were lucky to fill the room, get a free beer, sell a demo with a hand-drawn cover.

A strip of bars crouched on the corner of Saint Denis and Mount Royal and I'd go there knowing something would happen eventually. Le Luncheonette du Paris was across the street from Brooms, next door to that was The Spectacle, and upstairs was Red Rocket. Brooms was an old mason lodge with dark wood and stained-glass windows, ceilings so high you forgot they were there, tables shoved into the shadows. With Spectacle you had to duck your head at the door and go down into the earth. So dark you couldn't see who you kissed, so loud that when you ordered a beer you got a shot. Nights began by catching a show at Brooms then catching a DJ set at Spectacle. And who knew what you'd catch at Red Rocket—that was between you and your doctor.

Red Rocket was at the top of a Jacob's Ladder-type staircase that ascended forever, only you didn't end up in Heaven—unless your heaven consisted of canned dance tunes and having something slipped in your drink. Every once in a while some poor bastard went down the hundred-step staircase head first, ambulance already waiting for him on the sidewalk by the time he reached the street.

In Montreal, you could rent a room for a couple hundred bucks and work a few days a week. Then you were free to play music. Musicians did gigs by night, busked on the streets by day, did odd jobs, ran record labels, put up posters. Collected welfare checks or sold drugs. Cleaned houses, shingled roofs, bussed tables. I worked fast and careless, songs stuck in my head.

that girl suicide

Mont Royal was lousy with Caribbean men—they traveled in groups and smoked us up beside statues of angels and lions, blasting reggae on their portable stereos, laughing at a sky like an orange-and-pink melted popsicle, wet and heavy above the sparkle of the city. The mountain was a beautiful place to be stoned.

Jude and I swimming through the city, needing a lift. He said I should meet this girl. We went up into the dappled green of the side streets, a tide of cars rushing along like an aluminum sea. The place he took me was an old brick apartment building with fire escapes tacked to its side. A hundred crusty-eyed cats singing a capella on the step. Jude led me through the hall and knocked on a door at the end, the sun pushing through fleecy dust on the windowpanes. Someone screamed, "It's open!" from within, fighting to be heard over a record of guitar noise.

"It's Jude. I brought a friend," he yelled. He had to shove his way in—the entranceway was blocked with a hill of boots, a hundred variations of black leather.

The place opened up into a living room with a ceiling vaulted like a church, a window with a view of the bricked alley. The wooden floors were splintered and covered with cat toys, piles of clothes, miscellaneous garbage.

Pepper's arms were covered in scribbly old tattoos and she wore chunky gold jewelry wherever it would go. Her hair a mop of black bedhead. Her checkerboard spandex told me everything about her body in one quick look. She was beached on a velvet sofa and things had slowly accumulated around her: rolling papers, two black cats, an acoustic guitar with no strings, a stack of records, cassette tapes, a pair of leather pants, an industrial-sized bag of popcorn. The coffee table in front of her was buried by scales weighed down with scruffy tufts of marijuana, a coffee grinder, a packet of matches, an overflowing orange-and-brown ceramic ashtray, three plates with crusts of food, four mugs filled with congealed coffee and cigarette butts, a tube of lipstick, a black lace bra. Jude swiped a pile of clothes off a rickety kitchen chair and gestured for me to sit down.

When the record hissed to a finish, a thick silence fell on the living room. Pepper gave me a once-over. "What the hell kinda look you going for there, girl? Joan Baez circa sixty-eight?" She pinched a wrinkled joint in the corner of her mouth and squinted her eye as she struggled to get it lit.

I shrugged. "We must all be impersonating musicians today. What's happening with you? Elton John in ninety-one?"

Jude cleared his throat. Pepper gave this some thought. Then she laughed with her mouth open so wide I could see a missing tooth in the back of her head. "All right, all right, relax," she said. "Come sit next to me, sugar." She patted the couch and the cats skulked off to the bedroom at the back of the apartment.

"Where's Donny?" Jude asked, watching Pepper with an eagle eye as she weighed up our drugs.

"We broke up again so he's off with his band, probably getting fucked up and talking shit about me." She launched into a tirade about Donny, her live-in boyfriend, and his terrible band. Pepper's sentences were lost in "fucks," and "shits." I tried to get comfortable on a pile of damp paperback books.

When Jude finally got what we came for, he started for the door and didn't check to see if I was coming. Pepper gave me a sidelong glance. "How about you stay with me?" she said. "I'll make us dinner, get you high, and we'll see where the night takes us." I didn't know much about girls. Suddenly, I didn't feel like cavorting and roughhousing around in the dark. I wanted to get high with her and eat food with her and tell her my secrets and go out into the night, no longer a girl alone.

We ran down Parc Avenue in leather jackets and dirty jeans, the night blotted out by clouds spangled with streetlights. Pepper with a purse full of beer, our noses chunky from drugs. Donny was playing a show down at Brooms and even though Pepper told me she'd been banned from the place, for a reason she called A Long Story, we were going anyway. "They can't ban me. Don't they know who I am? I'm the best drug dealer in Montreal. I'm a badass bitch."

"I don't have any bus fare," I said, tipping the last of a lukewarm beer down my throat and putting the can on top of a trashcan for whoever wanted the ten cents.

"We're going to sweet talk our way on." Pepper sat down on the bench beside the bus-stop like a queen on a throne. "Or actually you're gonna sweet talk us onto that bus. You're prettier."

I sat down beside her and lit a smoke. "No."

"You bitch. Fine, I'll do it. And if they don't let me into that bar, I am going to fuck everyone up. They will regret the day they messed with me." Many people did.

The bus rolled up heavy with people and five minutes early. Pepper chugged the last of her beer in a panic. When we jumped up the steps, Pepper batted her heavily-mascaraed eyelashes and simpered, "Give us a ride. We're gorgeous ladies and it's dark out there." I hid behind her.

The bus driver shook his head and pointed back to the street. "Salut la visite," he said sarcastically. Pepper stood there dumbly. She didn't speak French. The driver pointed again at the street and yelled, "Aweille tabernak!" making us both jump.

I started back down the steps but Pepper struck a defiant pose. "If we get raped, it's your fucking fault." She shook her fist in the driver's face and then sashayed off the bus with dignity. As it pulled off without us, Pepper gave the driver the finger. "Fuck that guy. I'm getting us a goddamn taxi."

Pepper was thirty-something and had once been a beautiful waif—I saw the pictures. But she said she'd started smoking when she was seven years old. She used to be a folk singer in Saskatchewan, and that's how she'd met Donny, when he came through Saskatoon on tour with his band, Hotdog Special. Pepper joined the band as a tambourine player but was kicked out for trying to have sex with the drummer. She was a bit of a philanderer. She went from threatening to murder Donny to begging him to marry her every day. I never saw Donny when I came over to her apartment. I think he made himself as scarce as possible. I didn't know why he didn't leave her, but then they'd been together for eight years. They shared a record collection. If they split up, who would get the Moon Duo, the Hawkwind, the Spacemen 3?

Pepper, once untethered in the music scene after her expulsion from Hotdog Special, decided to start her own music festival called Garage Rock Fest. Everyone had a festival in Montreal. Hers would only last a year, and it had already burned to the ground before I met her, but she was always trying to get it going again. Her reputation had finally caught her. She spent winter mornings tobogganing down the mountain, high on drugs. She went to hiphop karaoke wearing pasties over her nipples that fell to the floor. She carried a butcher knife around in her backpack.

We got into the bar that night. The doorman was drunker than we were. And I don't know what happened, the lights were dark, the band was loud, and nobody cared that we were there. Then we were back on Pepper's velvet couch with Donny, bright-eyed and sweet, asking questions like, "How do you like the city?" Lines of burning drugs, hollering about bands, records scattered on the floor like plates at a wedding. The hours bleared away.

But Pepper eyed me all night and as I was leaving, wild-eyed and frazzled, into the morning, she hissed at me, "You better keep your hands off my man." And slammed the door behind me. We didn't speak for a week or two, but her cocaine binges often dovetailed into paranoia, I learned— it was just her way. I did not want to have Pepper for an enemy. She was the type who would blacklist your band from venues and tell everyone you had herpes. I juggled our delicate relationship with care, backing away slowly, like trying to get out of a gang.

come to the city

On the day I moved to Montreal, I took a taxi driven by a Moroccan man to my new apartment. He talked to me in French about miracles. I made the mistake of saying, "Je comprends français un peu," and he began to tell me stories in French. When he laughed, I laughed, pretending I understood his jokes. I picked out the words I knew, and pieced together what he told me.

He said his father was a doctor who biked around Fez helping out the poor and sick, while his mother spent her days praying for hopeless cases of blindness and other diseases I couldn't understand the words for. Her prayers were so strong that people were healed. He told me he came to Montreal through serendipity. When he dropped me off, he turned around and said in English, "Never forget you are immortal."

I've lived in almost every neighbourhood in this city, from industrial warehouses in St. Henri to blue-collar walk-ups in Point St. Charles, crumbling rooms in the Mile End above bagel shops. I used to have roommates, druggies and creeps, but got tired of getting my panties stolen or my cereal eaten.

Now I don't wear underwear and I live alone. I don't know how many years went by, four, five, six.

The members of the Crying Dads lived in a big mess of a house on the fringes of the Plateau. They were always trying to get rid of bedbugs. Taking in stray cats. There was always someone crashing on the couch, people who didn't know when the party ended. Drifters who didn't speak French or English.

Bamboo's parents were Japanese immigrants. He'd been born in the suburbs of Montreal and his parents named him Thomas. Thomas gave himself the nickname Bamboo. He spoke four languages: Japanese, English, German, and French. He spoke continental French but preferred the colour of the Quebecois dialect, hollering *ÇA VA* at people, roaring *JE PRENDS UN CAFÉ* when he wanted to get a coffee. And he only swore in Quebecois: *câlisse de tabarnak*, he shouted when he rode his bike into a pothole. The Quebecois made expletives out of religious props and rituals—as if offending a Catholic god was the highest crime. Bamboo said, "The symbol on the Quebec flag should be a hotdog wrapped in gold lamé, smoking a cigarette."

Jude refused to integrate himself because on his first day in Montreal an old white woman threw holy water on him and screamed, "*Vive le Québec libre! Retournez chez vous!*" Music theory was the only language Jude had an interest in anyway—there were no language barriers in music.

A Minor just had other stuff on his mind. He said, "What if all of our memories have been implanted into our brains like a computer chip? How would we know? If all we consider real is only what we can touch, then our memories and our pasts never existed." I would say, "But we were there." And he would say back, "Then it wasn't the past. It was only another now."

Like the rest of us, A Minor didn't mention his family. As far as anyone knew, he grew up in an anonymous Ontario town.

He liked to drink coffee on the streets in paper cups. That's where I ran into him most. He'd be standing there drinking a coffee with his headphones on. The street corners were our living rooms. There was something that stirred my heart when I saw him, an instinct to wrap my arms around him, to cook him a meal, to rub his hair. He reminded me of the San Andreas Fault, of the Marianas Trench. You couldn't picture him getting old, trying to raise children or pay off debt.

Polka Dot's real name was Henry. He'd grown up corn-fed in Alberta. The most rebellious thing he'd ever done involved a case of beer, a pickup truck, and the school mascot. He was always cracking terrible jokes. He'd make an excellent grandfather—sweater vests were designed with his body in mind. Polka Dot carried a picture of his three ribbon-and-tutu little sisters around in his wallet. They had names like Faith, Hope, and Charity.

His girlfriends wound up dumping him for jocks they met at the club while high on drugs and Polka Dot wore disbelief on his face like he had no idea what could have possibly gone wrong from dating girls of their calibre. The way they sparkled in their plastic jewelry, the way their Saint Catherine Street-shopping-spree shoes made them seem long-legged. He stared and stared. When the girls realized that no other musician was going to be taken in by their teen-fashion-magazine charms, they'd condescend to go home with Polka Dot. He'd been onstage, after all.

And when he was on the stage—how red his face got, how sweaty his curls, plastered to a face furrowed in aggressive concentration. Sometimes the Crying Dads performed in drag and Polka Dot dressed up like his little sisters, a sugar plum fairy in a too-small tutu with his balls hanging out.

The night of the gig with Milky Pete and the Mammograms finally came. We shlepped the gear across town on our backs and Bamboo saddled me with one of his keyboards. I wasn't sure if it was an honour or not.

"Remember," Jude said, "Milky Pete is on an international tour. That could be us, boys. It should be us."

People crowded out on the sidewalk under the lit-up marquee—the block letters said the name of an artist who hadn't played since before we were born. Etienne Tremblay or someone. Jude led us around behind the venue to the alley and brought out a tiny little bag of cocaine—he dug his keys in and shovelled out white powder, passing it around. Polka Dot pumped the air with his fist. Bamboo began jogging in place and singing *Purple Rain* at the top of his lungs. Jude lit another cigarette, muttering the set list over and over to himself.

Everyone became such silly fools when they did cocaine. The Beautiful Nothing. It was an Alice hole we threw ourselves down, snatching at curiosities that caught our eye only to toss them away a few seconds later. We told the same stories a thousand times.

Along the way to the green room, I lost the boys. The venue swarmed with people, a heat came off them in orangey rays of radiation. I went into the little concrete room backstage, crowded with old guitar cases, aluminum folding chairs, splintery wooden pallets, and closed the door on the droning buzz of voices. When I turned around, there was Milky Pete himself, and what I guessed must have been the Mammograms. They all had bald shiny heads and wore matching sports coats that smiled across their round bellies.

"Who are you?" sneered Pete. He sat on a chair while his band held court around him.

"I'm with the Crying Dads."

The Mammograms murmured uneasily. "We didn't realize we'd be sharing the green room," one of them said. They began shuffling around, arranging their gear.

"So," I said, by way of conversation. I was still standing by the door. "I heard you're on a tour."

None of them answered. I turned around to leave the room and collided with Polka, Dot, A Minor, Bamboo, and Jude. "Impeccable timing as always, boys," I told them.

Milk Pete and the Mammograms filed silently past us with their gear. "Soundcheck better be flawless," their leader instructed.

"Good grief," Bamboo said when we were all alone in the concrete room. "I heard their hit single is called Take Me to a Gay Bar."

"Don't they know they're in Montreal? Every bar is a gay bar," said A Minor.

We milled around nervously. Their nerves were making my own hands shake. Jude lit a cigarette even though he wasn't allowed, and hid it in his palm in case an outsider came in. "How old do you think the members of that band are?" he asked generally.

"Fifty-five if they're a day!" said Polka Dot. He drummed on the chairs with his sticks until Jude said, "Cease." Then he said, "Do you idiots want to be like them? Is that a goal you have in mind?"

"Yes?" said A Minor.

"No?" said Polka Dot.

"How do you want us to answer?" said Bamboo.

Jude stomped out his cigarette and growled. "Do you people even have goals?"

"Yes?" said A Minor.

"Definitely not," said Bamboo.

Jude stormed out of the room.

The gig went fine. Jude held the thing together, even if he was an overbearing father. They played so well he bought everyone a round of shots afterward. They played so well he brought out more cocaine. The Crying Dads ran through the venue shaking hands with everyone, sweaty and red under the lights. Milky Pete and his boys had vanished as soon as their set ended. It was just as well.

At the end of the night, I caught A Minor sitting at the bar with a drink, smiling thin-lipped at anyone who looked his way. "Wanna get some air?" I said in his ear.

He stood up quickly. "Do I ever."

We slipped away under the noise of the next band, letting ourselves be washed from the place out into the stillness of the night, a sky bruised by streetlights.

"Well…" I handed him a cigarette. You had to be cautious with those reluctant to speak—they were a flower that lost its petals the minute you picked it.

"Let's walk up here a bit," he said, shouldering his bass. He darted back inside himself whenever a crowd of shouting drunks shoved past. We walked through the narrow streets until we found a little square, some grass, a picnic table. He went over and sat down, started rolling a joint.

The cocaine and liquor had turned me conversational. "Do you like your life?" I asked him, lying down flat in the wet cold grass.

He drew hard on his smoke. "Jesus." Examined his fingers as if he wasn't sure who they belonged to. "If you want happiness you have to take sadness too. You can't have one or another. The happier you get the sadder you become—that's alchemy."

I could barely make out his profile in the dark, where he slouched at the picnic table. Airplanes moaned across the blackened sky and I could smell the wet of the nighttime grass. From somewhere the bark of a lonely dog. I wondered about this person who measured his happiness by the sadness that would follow.

"It's rock n' roll man. Nothing happens outside of rock n' roll. Or everything happens around it. I don't know."

We were in the rickety clapboard band-house, somewhere on the fringes of Little Burgundy and I listened as the lead singer of a band called Heavy Cheddar said, "I wake up sounding like Tom Waits when I talk on the phone."

The hours opened like a window onto chaos. Everyone gathered around the record player like a cave fire, the velvet curtains and gritty rugs, everything deep red and dark purple. Everything filthy. In the corner of the living room an unpaid journalist tried to get it all down. He was there from one of those publications where the employees wore their parents' clothes on purpose and called everything they did a Lifestyle. The uglier they looked, the cooler they became.

Heavy Cheddar had recently been signed to a record label in New York. They wore mouse masks when they played and draped the stage in dirty underwear. They threw processed cheese at their audience. I never recognized the members of the band, they all had long brown hair and half-beards, they wore the same jeans and sneakers. Heavy Cheddar's producer hovered proudly like he'd birthed them himself from his own innovative loins. "We're just trying to start a revolution," the singer shouted. "Wait, don't put that in there." He pointed at the journalist with his cigarette. "That makes us sound like assholes. We do want to revolt but the issues keep changing."

That night, the Crying Dads had opened for Heavy Cheddar and Hotdog Special. Afterwards the bands, the audience, the hangers-on, had made their way to the house. There were lines of white powder that could have been anything on the coffee table. Wine bottles filled the corners of the room like glass birds. Music made the windows tremble. The Crying Dads kept hollering that they'd played their best gig yet. "There's been talk of label interest," was how Jude put it.

I sat on a corpse of a couch in the corner, curious about the things that happened in the quiet, the private human rituals. But when you know too much, people usually retreat into the company of those who don't peek over their walls or unbutton their strategic facades. It was survival of the hippest.

Polka Dot had gotten into the spiced rum and was rendered useless. He leaned unsteadily against the wall, smiling vaguely. Jude stood by the record player, talking with someone in an exclusive sort of way about 7th chords. The members of Heavy Cheddar still wore their mouse masks and you could pick out the members of Hotdog Special because they all wore corduroy. I saw Donny and waved. He looked shell-shocked. He'd probably just escaped another near-death experience with Pepper, who was nowhere to be found.

I milled around. A Minor sat in the corner, a china saucer on his lap. His hands shaking. I went and sat beside him.

"Drugs smell like money. Cocaine smells like a five dollar bill," he said.

I helped myself to the plate. "Tonight was really wonderful you know," I told him.

And it had been. Polka Dot, Bamboo, and A Minor had worn matching bondage outfits they'd found at a sex shop on Mount Royal. It had been a real hit. But more than that, I loved their songs objectively. Their melodies made you call to mind your own memories, the way a good song should. I saw all my summers. I felt the sun. And everyone danced.

"B, there was no greatness there," said A Minor. He took back the plate and licked it clean. "It's like we have these moments of purity but we get lost in them and can't get out alive." Unlike Jude, who was all business and uptight direction, A Minor was a perfectionist in another vein—transparent as a new leaf, wincing under scrutiny and overexposure. "Maybe everyone only wants to have something to dance to. Maybe they don't give a shit. But I have this place inside me that I need to reach and if I can't make it there I'll fucking die." The kid was heavy as heaven. The drugs and thick syrupy alcohol weighed us down, like trying to run in a swimming pool.

"I have to go to the bathroom," I said, but I didn't. I went out to the front yard instead and watched the wind tear at the black trees, the bones of their hands trying to clutch the clouds and hold them. From behind me came the stale echo of music, voices fighting to be heard above the noise. I turned my face up to the sky, the wind moving cold across it and scattering loose rain. And I woke up alone in my bed.

happy nightmare baby

Pepper was in bed when I came in, the smell of cat piss smacking me hard in the face. She yelled, "Bring me my weed and my rolling papers."

There was only one piece of furniture in her room besides the bed—an old blue steamer trunk covered in crusty plates, fast food containers, a plastic bag, one red shoe. Strewn along the floor in a trail to the bed was a mess of clothes and cat toys. The sheets were half pulled off, revealing the mattress like a woman taking off her underwear. An ashtray rested on Pepper's belly. She was wearing sunglasses and a white fake-fur coat that made her look like a New Jersey hooker. The curtains were pulled closed and the room was dank and shadowy.

"Long weekend?" I asked, sitting on the edge of the sagging mattress.

"Don't even." She began rolling a phallic joint. "Donny told me it was over."

"Donny ended it this time?" I didn't tell her I had seen him at the party.

Pepper slid her glasses down her nose to direct a nasty look my way. Then she pushed herself up onto her elbows with great effort, the ashtray toppling from her belly and

43

spilling its acrid contents through the sheet. She ignored it. "Come out to the living room. I can't look at these walls anymore. I'm in a prison."

I followed her into the living room, with its coffee table covered in an ecosystem of crustified dishes. She pulled open the window and we leaned out of it, staring down into the alley with its network of sodden laundry and ratty telephone lines, pigeon gangs, stolen cars.

"I'm moving to Toronto," Pepper announced.

"You're out of your goddamn mind," I said, refusing the misshapen joint she kept trying to hand me. It smelled like a dead skunk and dirty socks.

"It's as far as I can afford to go. And I need to go. Every morning I wake up here in our apartment. And I sit here with all his shit, his junk, his notes to himself that say, *Write more songs. Work on guitar. Be a big fucking asshole.*"

"Where did Donny go?"

"Fuck if I know. If he doesn't want to be found then he's not worth finding."

"You're gonna get to Toronto and wind up living in a trash can with the budget you got."

Pepper let the smoke creep from between the gaps in her teeth, squinting out at the overcast afternoon. "I don't have a lotta options, princess."

Secretly I was glad for Donny, even as I sat in Pepper's trashed apartment. She was entertaining for me, but I didn't have to live with her. I ran my mind over her legacy—Jude told me stories of past tantrums and fits, her cocaine rages, the time she threw all of Donny's books into the street so that they were flattened by cars like roadkill. The time she shredded his leather jacket with pinking shears. I kept coming around because she had good drugs and good food, she was the kind of person with whom you could get properly fucked up, she was the kind of person you wanted to lie around with.

When Pepper got this way, strung-out and destructive, I sometimes tried to feed her lies like, *You deserve better,* and *It'll turn out all right,* until Pepper told me to shut the fuck up—I got tired of coming up with platitudes anyway. We both knew that things were shit. Pepper's life was more pockmarked with trouble than the face of the moon.

When she gave me advice, about my nebulous relationship with Jude, about making music, about hanging onto jobs, it was all the same. She said, "Fuck everyone. Fuck what they think." I warmed myself on the fires of her cross-eyed injustices. It was easier to survive when you were angry instead of sad. Pepper was angry about everything. Everyone had done her wrong—her shit list was more infinite than God's Book of Judgement. I got a kick out of her tirades when they weren't directed at me.

Pepper never did a thing to help her cause. Her comforts were vodka and Clonazepam, Xanax and Ketamine. Her version of growing up was more like growing sideways.

That afternoon, Pepper brought out the bottle of vodka and a little black saucer. "Black is better for keeping track of everything," she said. She rolled up a ten-dollar bill, purple and silly-looking, and offered me the first line.

The kitchen window was open so that a cold wind blew into the room. "First thing I'm gonna do as a newly independent woman is paint these walls. Get a new energy in."

"I thought you were moving to Toronto," I said, walking briskly around the room in a circle to get my blood flowing.

"Toronto?" Pepper began rooting around under the sink until she came up with a can of paint. She pried the lid off with her apartment keys. "Donny paid the rent on this place for the next month. I ain't going anywhere until I get my money's worth. Now help me fix these ugly walls."

Pepper poured paint thick as pancake batter into a cereal bowl and dunked a chewed-up paintbrush into its depths. "Now that I'm on my own," she said, "we gotta stick together. Don't let me get ballistic on you. We need each other. I think I have personality disorder. I feel things so much. But you're like my little sister. You try and copy me."

"I never had a big sister. Or any sister." I furiously lit a cigarette and sucked it down. Watched Pepper slop white paint across the walls, across band posters she hadn't bothered to take down. She painted over framed pictures. The white paint dripped and splatted onto the hardwood. "But I swear I don't want to be you."

Pepper passed me a paintbrush she'd also found under the sink and I dipped it into the paint, dropping dots along the floor. "Climb up onto that chair, would you?" she asked me. "I'm too heavy and I hurt my ankle falling down the fire escape yesterday. One of my stupid fucking cats tried to make a break for it."

I ascended the chair and it rolled like water beneath my feet. "Whoa," I mumbled and held onto the wall to steady myself, getting my palms wet and white.

Finally, it was too dark to see and even though Pepper turned on one or two scattered lamps, we'd lost our motivation. "Let's go lie in my bed," she said. She had a tiny lamp that projected stars onto the walls but she couldn't find it. "I've lost my stars, I've lost my stars," she kept saying, rolling around in her dirty blankets.

I put on Pepper's white fur coat and threw myself down onto the bed on my back, staring up at the ceiling and seeing stars anyway, even though Pepper couldn't find the projector. "I can't believe this is my life," I said, because the ceiling was the face of god and he was laughing and bearded and seemed to be around thirty-five years old. I wondered if our drugs had been cut with Fentanyl and if we would die. There were waves of doom and euphoria.

"Men always get to be the explorers," said Pepper from somewhere in the dark room. "They're the ones who get to go to the edge. Now here it's just the two of us. We're doing it."

But my body was decaying around me and the earth with it—soon everything familiar would be gone and I would arrive at a place where I recognized nothing.

The next day we were supposed to meet in the park beside the angel statue. The clouds rolled humidly across a grey and threatening sky, and I waited in the wind for a half hour before I saw Pepper hobbling along, carrying a bagful of samosas, crying.

"Saw that fucker with some new bitch, walking up St. Laurent proud as a parade." She shook under long sobs, her face contorted with grief and rage.

I patted her on the back and led her over to a picnic table. "Who are you talking about?"

"Don't you understand what I'm telling you, *puta*? That fucker has a new girlfriend. Who the fuck do you think I'm talking about? Donny, for fuck sakes. Donny." Pepper clumsily started putting together a joint, shoving her sunglasses up the bridge of her nose to hide the puffy slits of her eyes. "Where's my twenty bucks, bitch?"

"What? What twenty bucks?"

"For last night." She threw down her rolling papers and they scattered in the wind like translucent leaves. "I fucking knew it. I give you drugs, I let you into my life, and how do you repay me? By not repaying me! You thieving bitch." Pepper stood up and grabbed the fragrant grease-splotched bag of samosas, shoved her bag of weed into the pocket of her leather jacket.

"Aw, come on," I said.

"I bet Donny sent you to spy on me. Are you wearing a wire?" The wind caught her hair, sending strands of it out in different directions. Her sunglasses stood askew over her face, giving her the look of someone completely off balance. A seagull mocked us from the sky.

"Are you serious?" I sat there in the pinwheeling afternoon, not sure if I should be the one to walk away now, and quickly.

To herself, Pepper moaned, "I'm never doing cocaine again." And shoved her sunglasses more thoroughly onto her face.

"Can we get that on record?" I said. "Say it into the wire." And I pulled up my shirt, flashing her my bare belly.

Pepper threw back her head and let loose one of her raucous laughs, like a drunken pirate. "You're an asshole," she said and sat back down at the picnic table. "Want a samosa?"

I tried not to blow the powder from the end of the house key when I exhaled and when I inhaled, it burned up inside the tunnels of my cheeks, sending out flares from behind my eyes, my hands clenching with new energy. Pepper's soft round body, constrained by black clothing, pressed me up against the bathroom stall. There was a smell of bleach and piss. A walloping pulse of music beyond the walls.

Pepper was impatient. "Let's get out there already," she said, herding me out. The pale skeleton of my reflection caught in the flat mirror, two bruised eyes in a pale face. Pepper posed back at herself, pleased, and then turned her attention on me. "Girl," she said. "Nobody else is going to tell you this but that whole Uncertain-Librarian look…it's not rock n' roll. Get a haircut. Joan Jett." She fluffed her own mop-top and elbowed her way out of the bathroom.

I followed her into the crowd of uniformed youth done up in paisley and fur, hip hop T-shirts with the sleeves cut off, flannel shirts, big hats. Dancing under a net of red lights, we were important here in our small glories. Forget the Battle of Good and Evil, bring on the tall cans and titties, dime bags and distortion peddles.

Pepper had come to collect a band for her festival. We shoved our way to the back of the venue to wait out the opening band, a loud and screeching three-piece, and she yelled something into my ear but the noise took it away, out over the rows of heads bobbing in the dark red room. I went to the bar, fists clenched. Ordered a beer and got some weird cocktail. Pepper immediately got lost in the crowd. I pushed my way to the front of the venue, drink running down my wrist. Vampy girls in shredded shorts stared at the band from behind heart-shaped glasses, circlets of fake flowers in their curling-ironed hair.

The bleeding lights turned everyone's faces into rubber masks. I threw back the cloying drink. Bodies thrashed around me as if the person inside the suit of skin felt nothing. They threw themselves around like rag dolls. What was an elbow to the face, a foot to the head? I was never much of a dancer but everyone had a different way of feeling the music. I heard the most when I stood still. Some bands gave people shit for not dancing like maniacs and maybe they were right, maybe I was not free enough.

These scenes were a Who's Who. Same booze, same bands. I saw Polka Dot, A Minor, and Bamboo launching themselves from the lip of the stage. Jude off to the side nodding his head critically, probably trying to discern if the guitars were in tune.

When the band finally strutted offstage, spraying sweat like dogs from a lake, Pepper turned up. "Stay close, ya floozy," she said. Canned dance tunes came on while the next band unpacked their equipment up on the plywood stage. "You're not gonna believe these guys. They call themselves Ricochet Bonanza. Whatever."

I saw the band's frontman testing the microphone with the sound-man, their voices bouncing back and forth across the bar like they had tin cans strung between their houses. His dark hair hung down over his face, skinny arms smudged in old tattoos like a sailor. Under the heat of the lights he seemed to have an aura around him, like he was surrounded by smoke. That would explain the throng of succubae at the front of the stage, wiggling their asses to practice for the coming songs. I waded to the side of the room and climbed onto a stool to observe in anonymity.

Pepper noticed me and came over. "Ricochet Bonanza are a bomb about to go off. If I bring them onboard for Garage Rock Fest, shit is gonna explode. I'm a goddamned ambassador. Everybody better bow down." Pepper, the musical Jesus Christ. She'd done too much cocaine, it had gone to her head. "There's Donny with my weed. You wanna smoke one?" Asking out of politeness but she knew I didn't smoke. I already had enough trouble trying to come up with things to say.

Ricochet Bonanza was as she predicted though. Pepper at least knew music. Flammable levels of sound rose and fell like a wave. The man with the guitar, the one I'd been watching, shook like he'd been electrocuted. His guitar screamed into the crowd, the drums behind him bristling into rippling fills, slapping at the air like clapping hands.

"I want to have your fucking baby!" a girl screeched at him as he threw himself to the stage, fornicating with his guitar, as if oblivious to their swooning. The set combusted in a climax of guitar feedback, everyone sweating and red in the face. He threw down his guitar so hard that if it'd been a body he'd have broken its collarbone. And then the band swaggered offstage, adrenaline puffing up their chests like birds.

Pepper ran over. "Am I the fucking best or what? I know how to find 'em. Everyone owes me the biggest fucking thank you."

"Who's the guitar player?" I swished around a mouthful of flat beer, trying to sound casual.

"Take a number bitch," she said. "I've had my eyes on that one for months. If I can ditch Donny for a night, he's mine."

"I thought you guys were getting married in Vegas next month."

"Fuck Donny. I can't take one more minute." She'd be madly in love with him again tomorrow but tonight it was territorial pissings. "Besides, I heard that man fucks everyone he gets his hands on so don't get sentimental. He tattoos the names of the women on the inside of his thigh. He's got six illegitimate kids. Anyway, he's into me." She rubbed her nose of the thin cocaine mucus trickling out. "Last night he came over to get some drugs and we wound up talking for hours." She sighed, love drunk. "I can't wait to get my hands on that cock."

"I'm going out for a cigarette," I said.

A handful of us stood around in loose circles outside the bar, waving vaguely to acquaintances, flicking cigarette butts into the street. Smoking gave me something to do with my hands. I ignored an old man in freshly peed pants as he did a little dance in front of me, asking for a quarter, for a kiss.

And then I knew he was there. Whatever he emanated I felt on a primordial level. Turning slowly around, I saw him rummaging through a cigarette pack. "Got a light?" he asked me. Wasn't that just like a beautiful person—always in need.

"Nope," I said.

"Can I use your smoke then?"

I handed over my cigarette and watched him press its ember to the tip of his own smoke until it ignited in a blue feather. Exhaling up at the sky, he fell silent—as if passing me an obligation. I almost didn't want to say anything out of spite. We stood in a sphere of ambient city noise. The dark and vivid night, people calling out to each other as they went from place to place.

"Good show," I said at last.

"Thanks," and he sort of smiled, victorious. Then, "you'd be beautiful in the snow. With it on your eyelashes."

I stared at him like a bullfrog and laughed, a loud ridiculous sound directed at the whole night and everyone in it. How many women had he gotten out of their clothes with lines like that? I took a long drag on my cigarette, refusing to bat my snowless lashes. Montreal was a bad influence on people—it made them think they were romantic. Did he try and put his hand on my waist? But the bar emptied then, bodies surging around us in jostling mayhem. His many friends yanked him off and I stood there letting the people fade away until I was alone again. Trying to decide if he'd gotten me or not.

"The fuck was that about?" Pepper stormed over to where I stood under the awning of a closed shop, ducking under the teeth of the wind. "I saw you, bitch. Out here talking with him."

"Him who?"

"You know who." She put her hands on her hips, glaring up at me. She was a foot shorter than I was, a little Tasmanian devil of drama. "I should have told you this sooner. I fucking hate you. I've hated you for months. You don't know who the fuck you are, so you're trying to be me. You think you just gotta show up and be beautiful and the rest'll come easy. But you don't know a goddamn thing. This is my fucking scene and you don't belong in it. We're through, you and me." She came at me, closer and closer until I was backed against the glass door, cold as a kiss.

I said, "You don't know a thing about me."

She cackled out at the empty street, a laugh of anger. "Please. Bitch, you're no mystery. You're just as manipulative as anyone else." She had me penned in. I could feel the heat of her rage, smell the booze in her mouth. Her eyes glinted hard in the orange streetlight.

Around us the sidewalk was deserted. The sounds of an unknown band echoed out into the night, empty as a tin can. The smallness of my world came down heavy on me.

"I'm going home," I told her.

"You go on then and get the fuck outta here. Stop riding my coattails. Taking men I like."

"Donny thinks you only like one man," I said over my shoulder.

"Fuck Donny and fuck you!" But the wind took her words up and away.

"See you around, Pepper."

"You better hope not. I'll break you in two!"

I stepped into the wind, neon lights against the sky like a prison break.

"B, wait for us." Polka Dot and A Minor came jogging up the sidewalk behind me and I stopped to let them catch up, slung my arms gratefully over their shoulders. We began to walk in a clumsy line, passing no one. The streets were empty as a stage.

"Where's Jude?" I asked.

"Aw, he's back at the bar planning our futures with the sound man," A Minor said. "I saw you pissed off Pepper." He was red-cheeked from beer. I liked him that way, free of cares.

"Not that it's hard to do. That woman has lost the plot," said Polka Dot.

"Takes one to know one," I reminded him.

We turned onto my street, brutalized by Montreal construction crews—they came back every year wearing neon vests to stand around smoking, swearing. They'd destroy everything so they could come back next year and do it all over again. Orange pylons had been thrown up into the tree branches and scattered across the broken road. We picked our way through the ruins.

"And I saw you talking to Sam. Isn't he one crazy mother?" A Minor skipped along, trying to ferret out details.

"What are you boys, a gossip column? I don't know no Sam." But I felt a little hitch in my guts.

"Sam. From Ricochet Bonanza," Polka Dot said. "I was peeking from the bar. Anyway, I've heard some weird shit about that guy. I heard he did so much acid that he thought he was a glass of orange juice. They had him propped up in a padded cell because he was terrified he was going to tip the fuck over. That is actually a story I heard."

I rolled my eyes. "That's your classic acid myth. Let me guess. He also jumped out of a window thinking he could fly."

"Yeah! That's right!" An expression of genuine concern came over his face. I wanted to pinch his chubby cheeks. He said, "You're in love with him aren't you?"

"I disapprove, if you want my opinion," A Minor added.

"I'm not. And I don't." I reached my apartment, a walk-up with florescent foyer lights, gold letters of a woman's name painted across the glass doors. It would be morning soon. "Goodnight, boys. Try not to listen to those stories, they're no good for you." But I went inside smiling a little to myself, I couldn't help it. I was free of Pepper and things would keep happening, like the coming days were Christmas presents and all I'd have to do is wake up and tear off the paper.

punks in the beerlight

"What are we listening to?" Jude came into the jam space and saw Bamboo, Polka Dot, and me sitting on the dirty couch, A Minor cross-legged on the rug. It had been evening when we arrived but it was easy to lose track of the hours in a room with no windows.

"John Cage," Bamboo said proudly.

Jude unpacked his guitar, came over and kissed the top of my head, which made the boys howl and smooch the air to show what they thought of our romance.

"Only a white man would record silence and call it music," said Jude. "Turn that arthouse shit off and put on some Dexter Gordon. Someone who isn't afraid of notes. I got one phrase for you: The Emperor's New Clothes."

"The Emperor's New Clothes? That's the majority of popular bands," I said. Jude whipped around to examine my face, sussing out my motives for speaking against his opinion. But I was drowned out by Bamboo and Polka Dot, both of them hollering their points of view while a saxophone swallowed the silence.

A Minor told me he was playing a solo gig to make a little extra money and he got me on the bill. I'd been playing a few little shows here and there, opening for bands in empty bars, sometimes playing a gig with Jude.

Montreal had no preference who was on the platform, the Davids or the Goliaths, the rock stars or amateurs. Which meant I wasn't anything special for standing on a stage and strumming a guitar but at least I was getting in some experience. I stood on the same piece of raised wood as artists so great you said their names with awe. And still I got up there.

My last show had been crammed inside the vaulted room of a cafe, spider plants in the windowsills, milk jugs made into lamps like phosphorescence, half-empty bottles of wine shoved in my guitar case. I promised to try and play something pretty. I would only fuck up a few times. Every time I got onstage it felt like I was headed to my own execution. Sometimes I made it out all right. Other times I fucked up gloriously and it was all I could do to finish in a blaze of helpless frustration. When I stepped onto plywood bar stages under blue lights, the invisible audience rippling in the dark like a bedroom monster, tremors ran through my fingers, the subtle thrum of the planet's vibration shaking me up. I hated performing. I hated being watched. But I did it anyway. Every time I went onstage, it was another exposure, an admission of "this is what I sound like when I'm alone."

It was Tuesday at the end of autumn and the weather was crazy, purple-black clouds wrestling heavily in the sky. At any minute it'd all come crashing down on our heads. I was too cool to carry an umbrella. The people of Montreal had been running around confused in shorts, waiting for the bottom to fall out—we'd go from T-shirts to parkas in the span of two days and no one equated our fragmented behaviour to the unstable weather—it was too obvious.

"I met a woman," A Minor told me as we walked through the sloping streets of the Plateau up into the Mile End, taking side streets and alleyways.

"You don't say." I elbowed him in the ribs and passed him the tall can of beer. "A woman?"

"A woman. She's twenty-nine."

"An older woman." I kept my eyes on the shifting clouds.

He told me she graduated from Columbia and was about to take a trip to Lamu and wanted him to come along. She thought he needed to become "stable," he said.

A Minor was constantly being taken under the wing of older women trying to mother him. I guess I'd been guilty of it myself except I liked to think I was less of a dictator about it. "Might as well get a condominium and a credit card while you're at it," I said.

"Acting like skids and hood-rats doesn't make us more sincere."

"Sure it does." I swigged the dregs of my warm beer and tossed the can to the sidewalk where it made a flimsy sound. I already resented this woman and had only seen her from a distance at one of the gigs. I remembered her haughty expression. How beautiful she was. Not beautiful in the way that I thought I was beautiful, with my eyeliner, cigarettes, hair knotty because I didn't know what was supposed to happen with it.

Charlotte was beautiful because she had access to things I didn't. She'd read all the books you're supposed to read if you want to be an intellectual. She knew how to navigate the strata of social accomplishments. My knowledge was how to survive with not enough. Sometimes the world felt like a hotel lobby—everyone else peacefully sleeping in king-sized beds while I could only make it as far as the bar. I couldn't imagine the psychological freedom she must have had from being able to buy a plane ticket to anywhere on a whim. The only ticket I'd ever bought was a few tabs of acid.

I couldn't imagine paying for university or having a well-stocked fridge. I could barely make rent.

"She's a real lady," A Minor said as we trucked our heavy gear up St. Laurent Boulevard. "I hope she doesn't try to change me though. Maybe I need to change but I don't think it's remotely possible. I'm a train wreck. Choo-choo! All aboard the crazy train."

"You create your reality with your words you know," I warned.

"It's going to rain," he said, holding out his hand. The sky immediately split open. We walked faster. Within a few seconds we looked like we'd jumped in a lake.

"We're gonna drown," I yelled over the roar of the rushing water.

"One day we'll remember this and have a story to tell. When we're famous musicians with tour busses playing the international festival circuit. We'll talk about how we used to lug our gear to shitty bars in the pouring rain."

"You even know where this shitty bar is?"

"I think we're lost. We have to backtrack a couple blocks. Fuck. Where's our limo?"

We stopped to get a bottle of cheap wine at the dépanneur and slugged it back as if our lives depended on it. We stashed the remainder behind a dumpster when we finally reached the venue somehow, squinting under hammering sheets of heavy rain. The bar was an old fire hazard with blue-and-red tiled floors. Garish neon lights emphasized a row of slot machines jangling with lost quarters from the back of the room.

We hung up our sopping coats and shivered in the air conditioning, leaving puddles along the floor. We'd probably get electrocuted onstage. I bought us shots of whiskey to warm us up.

There were five drowned rat-types hanging around the bar, nursing drinks in flimsy plastic cups. I haggled with

A Minor and got him to take the opening set. We kept running downstairs to drink our wine and smoke cigarettes then running back upstairs to drink pitchers of beer. I was suddenly blind drunk.

A Minor got onstage with a mangled acoustic sourly out of tune. I'd never heard him play anything but the bass in the Crying Dads. He began smashing away on the little guitar, growling about freight trains and leaving home, the usual stuff.

I noticed a bearded flanneled man hunched over the bar. He was sipping a stupid looking cocktail and scowling, accompanied by a woman who gleamed in red lipstick. Their jackets were nice and dry.

"Could have tuned that guitar," he muttered to his accomplice, who chuckled knowingly.

When it was my turn to play everything became clear and sharp instead of sloppy with drunkenness. I set up my pedals and watched them blinking up at me like I was about to land an airplane. My fingers operated on their own and I felt a rush of gratitude for muscle memory. I sat back inside myself watching the half-dozen people watch me.

I was fine for the first few minutes but when the nerves hit me, my hands started shaking uncontrollably. Gripping the guitar, I plowed on, counting down the songs until I was free. Before my hands could shake themselves right off my wrists I finished the set to a thin pocket of applause. Then ditched my guitar and headed straight for the bar to drink away the adrenaline.

The bearded man sidled up beside me. "That wasn't half-bad," he remarked. "Lazy vocals, though."

"Drunken vocals more like it," I slurred. I vaguely remembered drinking a beer onstage.

Beard pressed a vodka into my hand. "Rock and roll," he said sarcastically. "What do you call that stuff you were doing up there?" he asked.

"Music, I guess." I used the bar to keep me standing up.

"But what are you? Indie-rock? Shoe-gaze, minimal post-punk?"

"What?" I scanned the room for A Minor.

He smirked. Instead of making eye contact he stared at my earlobe. "I want to know how you're marketing yourself."

"I'm not," I said, slamming back the drink he'd given me and throwing the cup on the ground.

He scoffed. "You're not getting up there because you don't want attention. That whole scornful-musician thing is so passé. I'm only trying to help you out. I do music marketing."

A Minor finally swept up to me, arms outstretched. He was hammered. "Darling! Let's get the fuck out of here!"

"Calm down." I patted him on the head.

"Me? I'm cool! I'm a cucumber. I'm a fucking honeydew melon! Who's your friend?" He pointed into the bearded man's face, almost took his eye out.

"A music marketer," I said.

"You market music?" He was too drunk to talk in a normal decibel. His pupils pointed in opposite directions. "Are you in the market? In the market for music? Shit, I'll sell you some fucking music. Bargain basement prices. I've tailored the tunes specifically for adult diaper commercials."

"I liked your *friend*'s music," the man said, struggling to maintain composure. The woman with the lipstick flirted with the bartender.

A Minor tried to give the bearded man a jovial punch on the arm and got nothing but air. "Who doesn't like her songs? She could be the next Celine Dion! Or Avril Lavigne!" He grabbed me around the waist, dancing me in a misshapen circle. I tried to push him away but wasn't successful and we went thrashing around the room.

Beard wore an expression of profound disapproval. "Take my business card okay? There's a phone number on there. You can use those numbers to call me. On the telephone." He said it as if he'd come from the future and had to explain what a telephone was. I grabbed his card and shoved it in a pocket.

"I can handle it, thanks," I said.

"My heart will go on!" A Minor screamed. I grabbed his hand and hurried him down into the streets that had been washed clean by the rain.

nitemare hippy girl

Infatuation could lead you off a cliff and you'd go over the edge with butterflies in your stomach thinking, "Look at me, look at me." The blues kept me awake. I wondered how other people kept their cool when I felt like I was being torn open every day. Who'd be the first to get on their knees, to open their mouth, their shirt, expose their neck for the blade?

Polka Dot had been bartending in Notre-Dame-de-Grâce and met a girl named Lisa, who had a band called Real Fish—she was the singer. She brought in Jude to play guitar, and asked Polka Dot to be her drummer if he'd get her band a weekly slot at the bar. After Real Fish secured the slot, Lisa kicked Polka Dot out of the band—his purpose had been served.

In bed, Jude and I passed a cigarette back and forth and only our fingers touched. The square of night that came through on us was studded with streetlights and the shine of passing cars below.

"Lisa said Polka Dot had to go," Jude said plainly.

"But she wouldn't even have that slot if it weren't for him."

"Lisa is ambitious and I respect that. You can't keep musicians out of sentimentality. He's a weak link."

"Or a rung in a human ladder."

Jude scowled and got out of bed, found his shirt on the floor. He never stayed naked for long.

I stayed in the sheet. "What about the Crying Dads? I thought you were recording an album."

Jude snorted. "Yeah right. Those bozos equate band rehearsals with benders. You know what happens every time I call a jam? Polka Dot gets a bag of coke and Bamboo gets a two-four. Besides, Lisa aced an audition with *Microphone Idol*. Her work ethic is incredible."

"Isn't that the reality show about who can sing the loudest? That shit has the artistic merit of a poutine."

I met Lisa once, when Jude brought me along to a rehearsal—they jammed at her parents' house in the suburbs. The house had pink carpets and gold lamps, a white brick fireplace, plastic venetian blinds. Real Fish mostly played covers by The Beatles but they threw in one or two originals, funk and R&B. They had a keyboard player who rapped.

"Who's this?" Lisa asked Jude the night he brought me. She'd dressed up for the rehearsals, orange lipstick, a long polka dot dress, her dreadlocks wrapped in a scarf. I sat on the edge of the pullout couch next to the television and sneaked baby sips from Jude's flask.

"She won't distract us," he assured her and plugged in his guitar. Lisa turned down the volume on the television. "My show airs tonight," she reminded Jude. "My mom made dinner but I didn't know you were bringing someone else…. There might not be enough."

The rapping keyboard player tinkled out a few notes to break the tension.

Jude said, "She won't stay long."

From the rectangle window, level with the frozen ground, I could see the snow coming down like shredded paper from the sky.

"Then let's not waste any more time," Lisa said, adjusting her microphone. "I just wrote a new song called *I Want Your Man.*"

I panned away from the basement in the suburb, on the road with the box houses. Past the highway back to the city, and out again. The rivers, the forests, the province. To the sea.

Lisa moved swiftly through the ranks of *Microphone Idol.* I went down to the bar where Polka Dot worked; Bamboo, A Minor and me, we sat there sipping beer through the tail-end of that long wet winter. The bar played endless episodes of the reality show, judged by a bloated bull-frog named Trevor Lajoix who'd made his career in the eighties with guttural French rock songs. More recently, he was known for getting trashed in bifteks and reliving old glories. He was a national hero. He wept openly when Lisa strutted across the stage in long hippie skirts, screaming a soulful rendition of an Édith Piaf ballad, her voice undulating spasmodically. Everyone in the bar clapped for her televised effigy, as if she could see their adoration from wherever she was.

I slouched on the countertop, watched Polka Dot mix cocktails in a silver shaker. A Minor sat mutely, staring into the depths of the bar, the dark wood, the stained glass, paintings of ships. I hadn't seen him much lately, but Montreal winters made recluses of everyone. He'd be fine. Bamboo filled the silence anyway, telling me a long-winded story about the invention of the theremin and how he was going to build his own out of trashcans and cardboard boxes. In the excitement, he spilled his wine and had to sop up the mess with a brown paper towel.

"What are you going to do now that Lisa's kicked you out of the band?" I asked Polka Dot as Bamboo scrabbled around beside me. "Shame you lost the bar slot, that was good money."

"Don't talk about Lisa," Bamboo called up from the floor.

"Yeah, don't talk about Lisa," said Polka Dot.

A Minor said, "Who's Lisa?" And then went back to staring at the wall.

Polka Dot said, "People around here can't talk about nothing else. How professional she is. How ambitious she is. I don't want to hear her fucking name, got it?"

"All right, all right," I said. But I had a feeling we would talk about Lisa again.

we're a happy family

Jude and I didn't make music anymore. We made dinner, we walked around the neighbourhood. Sometimes he slept over. But we didn't know how to move on and we couldn't go back the way we came.

I played music alone in my room at night, watching the dirt-covered snowdrifts on the street turn to water, watching the spikes of ice fall from the branches and leave behind tiny green buds, little promises telling me I'd be warm again one day.

Sometimes I went for a drink with the boys. Sometimes there was a show. The days went all together and then away.

A Minor had been found ranting and raving on magic mushrooms in Fletcher's Field. He'd pissed his pants and had been awake for three days.

Jude scowled across the table from me at a diner, stirring cream into his third coffee. "Cops said when they found him he was saying time had stopped. That he was in some sort of loop. I went to see him up at the psych ward and that's what he kept telling me too." He took one look at my face and said, "Don't worry, he's not there anymore. He's at home. He was only in the hospital for one night and then they released him. He's good now I think. They gave him some meds."

"Don't you think we should try and track down his folks? Isn't there someone we should call?" I wished smoking in restaurants was still allowed.

"I wouldn't even know how to do that. Besides, I asked him to call his family himself and he got very angry. We're all just gonna have to keep an eye on him from now on. He'll be ok."

Where had I been? Those boys on the run in the night. As soon as it got dark they turned themselves loose on the city like it was an amusement park and drugs were the tickets they needed for the rides. I would hear their stories later and sometimes wished I had the energy to trail them through the hours and the dark streets, the alleys and parks. As they smoked and swore and danced and traipsed through the night, impervious to weather conditions or natural fatigue.

I remember being a teenager and running with boys like them, hanging out in bus terminals and skate parks, sleeping in hospital waiting rooms just to get out of the rain. Now I felt like a millionaire every time I slept in my bed. I was too weary to follow them out into the drudge of their wild nights.

Someone needed to keep an eye on A Minor though, even if that meant running through parks while he raved about time loops, pissing his pants from the shock of being inside his own head. It just couldn't be me.

don't mess with the messer

When *Microphone Idol* whittled down its competitors to two people, Lisa and another, Real Fish decided to have a celebratory gig at the bar where Polka Dot worked. He wasn't working that night so the two of us went together to show face. Bamboo and A Minor wanted to chase down drugs and girls, so Polka Dot and I left them to it. When we finally headed out into the night, I was sloppy drunk, like a big fat layer of ooze laid out on top of things I needed to get over.

The chilly night was crowded with Lisa's fans. Polka Dot and I lingered on the terrace with cigarettes, listening to the hiss of cars. Winter was on its way, the damp cold climbing inside my bones. I shivered as I smoked and spied through the steamed-up windows into the low orange light of the crowded bar. I could see Lisa hugging crowds of her fans, Jude holding his guitar so everyone would know he was involved.

"What's going on between you these days?" Polka Dot asked, and I knew he was talking about Jude and me.

"I don't think Lisa appreciates that I take him away from Band Time."

"You know what she said when she fired me? Well, she didn't fire me. Not to my face, anyway. She told Jude to tell me that they wanted to go in a more professional direction." He threw his cigarette into a dark puddle.

I said, "You're a good musician. But more importantly you're a good fucking person."

"I'm still not on that stage."

Reluctantly, we pushed our way into the bar, into the crowded depths of strangers, the smell of boots and sour beer, the floor slick with dirty water, the canned music blaring.

We'd come just in time to watch Lisa sashay up to the microphone and wrap her leg around its stand. She shielded her eyes against the sharp white lights, and could she even see our faces in the crowd? Jude climbed onstage beside her, tuned his orange guitar. "Thank you for coming to see us," Lisa called out across the bar. "We're Real Fish and let me tell you: we are *funky*, we are *soulful*, we are *real*." She humped the mic stand at every descriptor, and the keyboard player accentuated her words with a bleeping synthetic noise. "Now I got a song for you called *I Want Your Man*." She ran her tongue along her lips and away they went.

"You want him? He's all yours," I muttered. Polka Dot and I elbowed our way into the steaming heart of the crowd, the stench of pissy beer, spotlights on us. "Give me that bag," I said to Polka Dot.

He slipped the baggie into my hand and I pushed my way to the bathroom, into the narrow stall, sniffing powder from the edge of the ammonia-reeking sink and then blundered back into the crowd under the muck of noise.

Someone was holding up a piece of pink posterboard with *I Love Lisa* scribbled on it. Lisa ran her voice along a series of scales to display her vocal prowess, Jude shredding out an accompanying guitar riff. Lisa played air-guitar beside him.

I got pushed up against the lip of the stage, jaw tense, hands sweating. Under the seedy lights a man pushed his pelvis against my ass and shouted at me, "Are you single?"

"I want your man," Lisa reminded us.

Everything roiled around me, pixelated, swimming. "Who me?" I shouted back. How could I define my time with Jude to this stranger, who panted beer breath into my face like a dog. I could feel the nylon of his hockey jersey, his body pressed into me so that I couldn't move. All the elbows and arms and sweat and Polka Dot somewhere behind me and I couldn't move. "I don't know…" I said.

The man said, "Jackpot," and shoved his aggressive mouth against my lips, his teeth smashing into mine.

The band stopped playing, as sudden as a needle pulled from a record. My arms slack at my sides, Lisa stood over me on the stage, like a cat who'd had its tail pulled. The lights like an interrogation room.

The bar was loaded with an awful silence, the crowd murmuring and shifting uneasily. "That's my girl," Jude screamed into the microphone, and threw himself from the stage, guitar swinging around his waist, wielding his fists. Hockey Jersey held up his palms in surrender but the crowd pushed him forward, wanting a fight.

Polka Dot grabbed my arm, pulling me from the crush of people. "B, we have to go."

There was the street, same as it'd been only thirty minutes before, but now it was dark and distorted, how it spun and betrayed, streetlights running down into the gutter. I leaned against the side of the bar.

"What happened?" I think I said. "What happened?"

Polka Dot said something quietly but he was interrupted by Hockey Jersey, who'd followed me outside.

"You little slut." He came up into my face, this time not to force kisses from me. "You fucking slut, you told me you were single."

Polka Dot stood between us. I wrapped my arms around him from behind, using him as a human shield. Polka Dot said, "What rights does that give you? De câlisse, you piece of garbage."

"Your friend here is a fucking slut." As he walked off down the sidewalk, he spit a loogie like a raw egg at my feet.

Back inside, the band finished up their last song, a bawdy blues rendition of some standard, and the lights came up. Revealing spilled beer, smashed glasses, woolen scarves mauled in puddles on the floor.

My limbs full of sand, I lurched back into the bar. I had to find Jude and explain myself. He'd understand. He'd called me his girl. The smear of my brain cells across the night, the cognitive wind-down, I saw Polka Dot climb into a taxi. "Come with me," he said and I should have.

"You whore," Jude said when I found him in front of the bar. "You're a whore." The lights spangled in my eyes. A bartender shook his head at me, the keyboard player frowned at me as he put away his instrument and filed past. "How could you do that to me? How could you do that to Lisa?" Lisa stood behind him with her arms crossed, her lips pressed severely together.

I said, "I'm drunk."

"You're always drunk," Jude said. "You're a drunk whore."

The next day I woke early with a pounding headache. The day was sunless and humid, grey and ugly, my bed a ruin around me. I called Jude.

"I can't talk, B," he said. "I'm on my way to an emergency band meeting to talk about your behaviour last night. Lisa says you can't come to our shows anymore." He hung up.

A few days later, Bamboo told me that Lisa got signed to a label and promoted Jude from her guitarist to her new boyfriend. They moved in together the very next day and I didn't know it then, but I would hardly see Jude again. The city was like that. You could crawl all over it and never run into anyone.

keeping jive alive

"Boys, I'm getting too old for this," I tried to say, but my words melted away. I wasn't drinking and in place of that was smoking more cigarettes.

"You've changed, man," Bamboo said, snapping at his red suspenders absentmindedly.

"You're taking yourself too seriously," Polka Dot added. But he stared at his shoes when he said it.

We loitered around the fire escape outside of Blue Bread, a crusty loft venue and living quarters. But to imagine anyone living in the place was both fascinating and disturbing.

"Come on, B, let's put in an appearance before you die of old age," Polka Dot said, grabbing my arm. I relented because it was nighttime and though I felt old I was actually young. Drunken nights of debauchery were the only activity—if I wanted to do something else, I would have to do it alone.

We went upstairs and waded into the bodies and noise. The boys immediately vanished, leaving me stranded in that damp mouth of a gathering space. I stood around in the shadows waiting for something to happen.

In the middle of the main room someone had built a flimsy plywood stage a few inches from the blackened floor. Second-hand lamps shoved into the corners had red paper for shades—the light the colour of dirty roses, filling the place with pink gloom.

A DJ in a rubber mask and red plastic suit made experimental noises on their jimmy-rigged synthesizer and the crowd bobbed along like a bunch of dashboard dogs, complacent to the buzzing screams blaring from the stage. I felt ornery. I should have been at home knitting an afghan.

In the armpit-scented crowd, I spotted Bamboo and Polka Dot humping the legs of two girls in time to the dance beats. The girls had matching shaved heads and black lipstick.

I lit a cigarette to pass the time. Immediately, a lanky eighteen-year-old, hair greased back with cooking oil, sidled up. He was wearing a yellow fisherman's raincoat. "No smoking inside, Bro," he told me. "This is someone's home. Show some respect." And vanished back into the darkness.

I took in the beer cans clanking around my feet and remembered the bathroom with its mossy toilet bowl. Who's home was this exactly? Raincoat boy's? Across the room Raincoat was gesticulating aggressively at the door. Disgruntled that he'd called me Bro, I did not extinguish my cigarette but instead left the premises puffing emphatically and blowing the smoke at the ceiling where it would hang in poison rainclouds forever.

Once outside, I leaned against the brick wall of the venue and deeply breathed the city air. I was getting too old for these constant wall-leanings and DJ raves. But what followed these times? If something came after, maybe it wasn't meant for me.

he would have laughed

When the winter began to ravage the streets into salt-encrusted husks, I went inside and didn't want to come back out. Winter in Montreal was a heartless bastard. It socked you in the stomach, pushed you facedown on the sidewalk and rifled through your pockets. It was cruel, it overstayed its welcome. It fooled you with its pretty face so that you wouldn't notice its teeth sinking into your flesh. It took a person triple the time to get anywhere because you had to tiptoe over sidewalks slick as hockey rinks, thigh muscles tense from trying not to fall onto brittle bones. Days died in the darkness. I was exhausted by dinnertime.

After hiding inside for weeks, pacing my floors, writing half-baked tunes and flipping listlessly through books, watching the snow soap the windows until I couldn't see anything but white, I finally asked the boys to meet me at a café. As I walked down side streets, doubled over, the wind screaming its ghoulish whistle into my ear holes, I began considering a move to a warmer climate.

Bamboo, Polka Dot, and A Minor looked like they'd been considering the same thing. They hunched wretchedly inside their jackets, faces stiff and red, stomping and puffing in the blinding white afternoon, standing under the awning of the cafe as if it might protect them from impending hypothermia. The wind screamed and whipped its razor edge across our cheeks.

"Lovely day," Bamboo greeted me. He'd been trying to smoke a cigarette but the filter froze from the wet of his saliva. A Minor was already inside, pressing his face up to the warm window and making obscene drawings in the steam.

"I'm glad we're worth emerging for," said Polka Dot.

I took them by the arms and examined them for signs of change, it had been so long since I'd seen them. Winter had taken over my life.

Inside, we hunched over coffee cups, trying to get the feeling back into our fingers. Crammed in around the table on rickety chairs, our conversations lost under the screaming of the espresso machine. Muddy water and salt accumulating in puddles of sludge around our sneakers. We had too much pride to dress in parkas and ugly boots—we wore leather jackets and got pneumonia. We were idiots.

When the espresso machine stopped screaming, Bamboo said importantly, "We have news." He blew too hard into his hot chocolate and scattered whipped cream across the tabletop.

"Oh?" I couldn't feel my toes and the more I scrunched them up the worse it became. People kept coming in and going out of the cafe, letting in savage winds that came right for me.

"We got signed to a label. They're from Germany, so we're going on tour in Europe. Jude set it all up. The launch party was crazy, there was a creepy clown there making penises out of balloons, you know, because of our one song about the..."

"How come nobody called me?" I interrupted. I gripped my coffee cup until it scorched my fingers.

A Minor twirled his coffee spoon in his hair until it accidentally knotted and Bamboo had to pull him free.

"I thought you were hibernating or being a monk or whatever it was you said you had to do," Polka Dot said, rubbing his ears over and over. He probably had frostbite.

"But this is a big deal. You should've called." I sounded pathetic.

Polka Dot slung his arm over my shoulder. "All right. We're going on tour. We got signed to a record label. There. Now you know. We're going to get drunk at Heavy Cheddar's house tonight, wanna come? They're hosting a bunch of strippers from Toronto."

"Pass."

"See, this is why you're out of the loop," said Bamboo. "You're not around when stuff happens and then we forget you weren't around, so you get left out."

A Minor shouted, "Keep your head in the game! Keep your stick on the ice!"

But Polka Dot saw my face and said, "You're still our friend, B."

"Yeah, yeah, yeah. Don't worry about it," I said, swallowing the last of my cold coffee. "It was nice seeing you guys but I gotta get going." But the only place I had to be was my bathtub where I would spend the next three hours.

A Minor let us know in his own way that he was sad, but his sadness was beyond us. He was the type of sad person who got rip-roaring drunk and screamed nonsense until everyone around him felt awkward and crept away.

Like the night I caught him running into open traffic on St. Laurent Boulevard. I'd been in the bar across the street, trying to thaw my bones from the chill of spring, and spotted him dodging honking cars like he was in his own personal video game. I ran out into the hissing slush and grabbed his hand, pulling him onto the sidewalk. He barely recognized me.

"All right, chica. Take my hand! Take me to the other side!"

"Hey man, why are you running in the streets? Come on, I'll buy you a beer." I led him into the bar. Drivers shook their fists at us. I flipped them the bird. What the hell did they know about it.

A Minor was babbling—it could have been small talk but it flowed too fast, it was like he was singing. I tried to understand him but he wasn't talking for anyone's benefit but his own. I knew there'd been drugs and not enough sleep but what was the harm—we all lived that way.

I sat him down at my booth where I'd been reading a book over my drink, the table safe in the corner. I ordered two more pints off the barmaid who looked at A Minor like he was a dog in the supermarket. I gave her a dirty look. She scurried off and came back with two dripping amber glasses.

"You okay?" I asked him. Clearly he was not okay. But it was important to start there and then work our way up to the overwhelming and unexplainable. He sipped at his beer, his wet hair hanging in his eyes, his hands red and raw from the elements—he stared at them like he was trying to read a map.

"Are *you* okay?" His gaze snapped up so quickly I almost jumped. "More importantly, is that fucking guy okay?" He pointed at a completely normal man sitting at the bar in a button-down shirt, drinking a glass of white wine.

"What's wrong with him?"

"How can you ask that?" A Minor turned horrified eyes on me, pupils as big as mushroom caps. Instinctually I grabbed his arm and held it, as if the winds of crazy might blow him away. "What's wrong with him you ask? What is exactly wrong with a man like that? Well. I'll tell you. Just look at him. Look at him, goddamn it."

I turned as subtly as I could and tried to glance at him without making him turn our way.

"He sits there," A Minor waved his hands around in such a dramatic gesture that he almost wiped both our beers from the table, "and he is totally oblivious. He doesn't even KNOW!" He screamed the last word, banging both his fists down so hard on the tabletop that everyone in the bar stared.

"Take it easy," I shushed him, ignoring the frowns of the bartenders. I put my arm around his skinny shoulders. "You gotta chill out. Yes, the world is fucked up and we'll never afford to do anything more than cover the rent of our shit-box apartments and dream about the lives we could've had if we had rich parents and engineering degrees. We'll figure it out."

"But we haven't got time." He said it pleadingly, as if he was asking for more of it.

"Let's drink these beers and I'll walk you home." I figured Jude and Polka Dot might be able to handle this better than me.

"Alright, good idea. Yes, that's a good idea. Salute." And he grabbed his drink and smashed it into mine, practically chipping the glass and slopping beer absolutely everywhere. "Here's to that guy." He said it so loudly that the man with the wine tuned around to see. A Minor winked at him and slugged back his beer in two or three exaggerated gulps. Then he shook himself as if he were trying to shake off the last couple of hours. God knows what he'd been doing before I'd caught him in the middle of the road. "That was a fine beer. Okay. Sit tight. I gotta take a piss."

"I'll be here. But when you come back let's get the fuck out of this bar. Please." I realized then that I'd been sitting on the edge of my seat clenching my fists.

He stumbled up and jogged in the direction of the bathrooms. I watched him go with a sinking feeling, a metallic taste in my mouth. I probably sat there thirty minutes before it dawned on me that A Minor must have slipped out the back door and wasn't coming back.

A few days later, the sky was heavy with the kind of light that only came before sunrise. What had woken me up? A banging on my window, a scrambling noise. I clambered onto my knees, wrapping the blanket around me for protection. A Minor came crawling onto my bed with his muddy shoes, eyes wild as a raccoon in a trashcan. He rolled onto the floor, stood up, and brushed himself off. Lighting a cigarette, a philosophical expression came over his face.

By now I had pulled on a shirt and was fully awake. "All right. Okay. Hold on just a minute. You got mud all over my blankets." I was particular that way.

"Sorry about that." He blew a smoke ring that ended in failure.

"What the hell is going on around here? This is a goddamned intrusion." I stood up long enough to snatch his cigarette away and take it for myself. I figured it was the least he could do.

A Minor took in his surroundings as if he had finally realized where he was, and then climbed back into my bed with shoes still on, crumbling dried mud everywhere.

The open window blew clean cold air into my room. I wrapped the blanket around us and looked over at him, the crazy apparition.

"What a fucking night," he sighed, interlacing his fingers behind his head.

"Do tell," I yawned, all sarcastic.

"It's over between Charlotte and me. Not a thing I can do to salvage that mess." He stared up at the ceiling, scratching his chin. He appeared frazzled like he'd been up all night sticking his fingers in electrical sockets. The sky was turning the colour of wine-stained teeth. "She was having a party at her *loft*," he emphasized the word with disdain. "I went alone. Big mistake. It was all her university friends and people she knew from these political things. And there's me, the straight white male. They kept treating me like I was about to start humping their legs."

I massaged my temples subtly, the end of the cigarette dangling from the corner of my mouth. "Look, just give me the facts," I said. "If you try and hump my leg, I'll castrate you."

A Minor shuddered. "The world is not for me," he said. He jumped up, went to my record player, and put on Abner Jay. Coming back, he slumped into bed as if the action had depleted the last of his will. "I kid you not, B, they wanted my testicles. They wanted to make an example of me."

"Just tell me how the fuck it happened that you came to be tracking mud across my nice clean bed at this ungodly hour. Tell me why I shouldn't toss your raggedy ass back out into the streets."

"Be nice. I've had a stressful night," he said.

"*Oh Lord, I'm so depressed…*" said Abner Jay.

"A Minor," I said through gritted teeth.

"ALL RIGHT," he barged on. "I had a sheet of acid. I was gonna sell it at Charlotte's party until I realized it wasn't a party. They only wanted to listen to Boy George and talk about smashing the patriarchy. I wound up eating half a sheet by myself out of boredom. But it backfired and I got afraid. What do women see in me besides some fucked up kid they want to mother-hen to death?" He didn't wait for me to answer. "People don't care. They're black holes. I wound up sneaking back to the house. No one was home. I packed up all my shit, my guitar, everything, and started walking for the bus station. But then this car pulled up and the man inside asked me if I wanted to go to a party. We drove for a really long time. I have no idea where we wound up. Longueuil or somewhere. His party was a few teenagers sitting in a smelly basement. Nobody spoke a lick of English. Somehow, I sold the rest of my acid anyway and wound up sitting there for like three hours and then walked back to Charlotte's. By then, everyone at her place was wine-drunk and arguing about rape culture. She took me into her bedroom and told me I was a misogynist. Then she got out a pair of handcuffs and told me to punish her. It was all very confusing. I came here right away."

"I'm a regular block parent," I muttered. I closed my eyes for a second, but when I opened them again the sun was high in my window and my bed was empty.

I went down to the corner to see if A Minor was around and was surprised to find him. I didn't expect him to be predictable anymore. I expected he would be as hard to find as he was to understand. I walked over to where he stood leaning against the wall of a building, smoking and bobbing his head to music in his headphones as if nothing wrong had ever happened in his life. "Man," I said, walking straight up to him.

"Oh hey, B," he said, glancing distractedly up the street.

"What's going on?" I demanded.

He glanced at me, irritated. "Are you talking about the other night? I'm sure Jude told you *all* about it. Everyone has off-nights from time to time. No room for improv with that guy."

"I think it's probably a little more than that wouldn't you say?"

"No. I would not say. And I'm kind of waiting for someone here so…" he looked up the street again, harassed.

I refused to take his cue. Minutes passed this way with us standing there. He tried to pretend he was alone so I did that too. We took in the street. We watched the world go by. Horns honking, busses groaning, students in sweatpants rushing past us with their gleaming ambitious faces, going off to be doctors and scientists. Everyone carrying coffee cups and newspapers, beyond touching. No one could stop, they'd all wind up late. They'd be panicky and rushed, calf muscles cramping as they ran, ran to their destinations. But the street corner was our destination. We'd already arrived.

I studied A Minor without him noticing. The frantic way he drummed his fingers, the way he tugged at a strand of his long hair, his eyes darting. His face had grown so pale. He had probably lost a good ten pounds. I wanted to grab him and give him a good shake to see if that would break off whatever had gotten hold of his spirit.

Quietly this time, so that I wasn't sure if he even heard me, I said, "What's wrong with you?"

He said, "If I could dig down into the earth, past the outer crust into the mantle and the inner core, I could pull up all the things and examine them without flinching or looking away. Then I would be free. Which means I'd probably die because as soon as you learn everything about yourself, you die. That's why people hang on to their pain, because they think it's less scary than meeting death. Death can be found in freedom or freedom in death but because both are unknown, we hang on to the messes we've already gone through." He was staring straight ahead, at a man coming toward us. Anywhere between the ages of twenty-eight or forty-three, his slimy hair was greased back over a grey forehead, smoking a cigarette that looked like it had been plucked from a puddle.

He came up panting and said, "Thought we said to meet alone. Who's the chick? Your butt buddy?" He sucked on his teeth and looked me over.

A Minor ignored him and turned to me, his eyes calm and flat, his voice monotone. "I have to go," he said.

A week later I was riding the bus to the diner, obliterated by hangover and exhaustion, amazed that my body was able to sit upright, that my eyes were open. Luckily, I could show up there in any state. And did.

My phone rang. It was Bamboo. He never woke up until at least two in the afternoon. Keeping my forehead pressed against the cool glass of the bus window I grabbed my phone. "Bamboo? What are you doing awake?" Provoking him when I was hungover could be a good time. "Is someone paying you to be up this early? Have you been to bed yet?" I closed my eyes for a minute, dreaming of strong coffee and another life.

"Knock it off. Where are you?"

"I'm on the bus going to work," I said. And then I sat up straight. It was his tone of voice.

"You should get off the bus."

"Why?" I massaged my temples. Hoping it was just someone in the drunk tank or a stolen guitar.

I could hear Bamboo on the other end, breathing. "It's Ben." He meant A Minor. But nobody called him that. "He's gone."

"Gone where? I swear to Christ…speak plain." Everything churning around me like heavy water.

"Get off the bus so we can talk." I heard the scritch of his lighter as he lit a cigarette. "Ben is dead. He killed himself."

I pulled my phone away from my ear and stared at it. Stupid machine. And then suddenly I could only breathe in short gasps. People stared at me. I stared back until they had to turn away.

"B? Are you there?" I could hear him from far away on the phone. I wanted to take the call and throw it to where it couldn't touch our lives.

I jammed the phone back up to my ear. "What is happening?" I think that's what I said. I looked wildly around the bus but there was no one there who could help me. At the next stop I stood drunkenly, pushing my way through the doors onto the street. Everyone staring. I raised my middle finger over my head running down the sidewalk. I hoped they saw. I hoped god saw.

"He hadn't shown up to work," Bamboo was saying. He was still talking.

How were we supposed to know? He was us. How should we have helped him? And would he have taken our useless help? Would any of us take help? We wouldn't recognize it.

"How'd he do it?" The street screamed around me. I tore down the sidewalk. People gave me a wide berth.

"Wire from the balcony. Around his neck."

"Who found him?" My voice came out smashed in a trillion shards.

"Henry." The time for nicknames was over. Ben was dead. We would never be children again. "Henry found him last night. He'd been dead for two days."

"What...?"

"I don't know. Henry had to go home this morning. He says goodbye. I don't know what this did to him, but he said he couldn't stay here anymore. I guess everyone else is coming over to the house today. I don't know what else to say."

"I'm coming over."

We took the days in shifts. As if we were keeping a lookout. His dirty pants were still on the floor. He had a little tabby cat he'd kept secretly in his room that nobody even knew about. She'd given birth to six kittens in his closet. What a discovery that was. He'd left behind little messes like he was coming right back. We all unintentionally kept a vigil. We slept without resting.

When things got too heavy, there was the unexpected joy of a boxful of kittens. How like him to leave something like that behind. Our laughter caught us off guard. We cooked for each other, forcing ourselves to eat. It was unbelievably hard to do little things like take a shower, eat a meal.

Friends came and went, just to be in the house, to feel the leftovers of his presence. Charlotte never came, she was abroad. Jude and I moved around each other, not talking.

The boys stayed drunk, high, obliterated. They wanted to do cocaine all night and talk about his mannerisms and jokes, the stories they had. They wanted to talk about the day it must have happened, where they had all been, what they'd been doing. They talked about his family. The police had called them. Thankfully, none of us had to do it. There would be a funeral in Montreal as a gesture for his friends—the parents were to arrive in the next couple of days.

Childhood friends, girls he'd fucked, second cousins, they all came out of the woodwork, trooping through the house, offering up their regrets as if we could use it for something. I wanted to ask them, "What is this for?"

Every time my mind started to shift out from under the patterns of sadness something dragged me back. I was a dog on a chain with limited room to run—but why would I run even if I could? I owed him this time. I should have never left him alone for a goddamn minute.

Their band fell apart immediately. After a few lost weeks, they tried to have a jam but it ended in disaster. They'd been told by some producer to kick Thomas out of the band. Jude didn't break the news kindly.

"You're fucking cheesy," he said plainly.

"And you're a jazz school drone." Thomas wore a face like a crumpled paper bag. Gone was the old Bamboo. He threw his pedals so savagely into a duffel bag they sounded smashed to pieces. "Just because you wank off all over a fretboard doesn't mean you're being creative." He started for the door of the jam space but Jude stopped him with a fist to the face.

The two of them fell to the floor in a violent tangle of arms and legs. I grabbed Jude by the hair and yanked hard. That broke them up.

"Knock it off," I shouted. "He would have hated this."

"He," said Jude, spitting blood onto the floor, "fucking killed himself."

Thomas stared at me with liquid eyes, searching for answers in my face where there might be something to save him. In the seconds that followed, when all of us stood around with our own thoughts, and I couldn't fix anything and that came to be understood, Thomas stormed from the room. This time no one stopped him.

I hadn't seen anyone in weeks, had been hanging blindly around bars and street corners as if the days were still the same and I was still the same.

The minutes were monkey bars and I swung from one rung to the next trying not to fall below. The funeral was nice but it was also a fucking disaster because it was the funeral of our friend. The family all bent over in pews at the front of the church. Jude and Thomas quietly filed in at the back with a bunch of others, pale-faced and blinking. There were more people there than we expected. We warmed ourselves from the crowd like we were homeless, standing around a barrel fire.

His parents had come to town the day before, and called Thomas wanting to come over to the house to see where their son had lived. I came too so we could clean up, put on a good show. Make the place seem like a nice space where their son had spent time. Nothing disturbing, nothing bad. We did dishes, swept, straightened up the house in silence, shuffling around with a broom or an armload of laundry. It was the first time we didn't have music playing.

I went into Ben's room to make up the bed. Nobody had been in there yet, not really. I touched his pillows, played with the kittens who lolled around the bed meowing and wrestling, the mother cat beached on a pillow. I sat on the mattress with its ratty blanket and smells of hair and skin. I heard the door creak and Thomas stood there, an expression on his face like he'd lost his hands. An unlit cigarette forgotten in the corner of his mouth.

"B," he came in, sitting on the edge of the bed. "Don't. We're going to be okay."

"No, we're not," I said. "We're going to be fucked up." I wiped snot across my face, didn't care, could barely see through the slits of my eyes. He passed me his smoke, lit it for me.

Having to do normal tasks like getting toothpaste from the drug store was impossible. I couldn't touch my guitar. Couldn't put on a record. I knew every inflection of his voice, I heard his stupid jokes and the way he sang his stupid songs.

"How is this a real experience?" I asked Thomas. As if he knew more than me.

He shook his head, helpless as I felt. Neither of us could keep sitting there in such a crushing shadow so we stood up and continued on.

How suburban his parents were, with their greying shopping centre hairdos, windbreakers, jeans and sneakers. Painfully polite, they followed us around the house, peeking into the kitchen with its mismatched chairs, smells of cigarettes, recent cleaning products.

The parents wanted to go into his bedroom alone. We sat on the couches and waited, could hear the mother crying. I blinked my eyes very hard.

Later, we sat around the living room. The mother told us what he was like when he was little. She said he'd been scared of dogs. He loved to take baths. He said he'd wanted to be a teacher when he grew up. She tried to tell us funny stories but laughter was a trick played on us now. Thomas and I shook their hands when they left, like tour guides.

In the days that followed, I only wanted to do things that involved him in some way. I wore his T-shirts. I found homes for all the kittens but Thomas kept the mother around the house. She still slept on Ben's bed. I hadn't been back to my own apartment in over a week. The hours dragged themselves along the ground.

the dust blows forward n' the dust blows back

It had been a month since the funeral, time a blur of nothing. I went for long wanders through the alleys, slept too much, watched terrible movies.

The summer had become a carnage—there'd been casualties. In the hot climax of an inner-city summer people stopped sleeping altogether. They neglected their diets, living on poutine and cheap beer, dépanneur wine, cocaine. Who cared. Who would stop us. We'd spend September facing the consequences.

A Love Supreme

Half-jogging down the alley with my guitar flapping heavily on my back, blasting *A Love Supreme* through my headphones to clear away impurities. Trees stretched above the alleyway in a patchy ceiling and beyond that the sky, grey with coming summer rain. Kids kicked a deflated soccer ball and stared as I swooped past. You could wind through all the back lanes of Montreal and never see anyone but children and cats. Vast murals and graffiti plastered onto wooden garage doors, double-panelled like old barns, words as art.

Putting my foot up on an eroded stair to tie my bootlace, I noticed the purple doorway. I imagined the door was a portal to a place with palm trees and white highways. But then the door opened and I was eye-level with someone's black pant leg. There was a smell of cigarettes and dust and, beyond the open door, a glimpse of a dark hall.

A love supreme, a love supreme.

He said "Excuse me," like he was used to finding strange women tying their laces on his doorstep. He said excuse me not to excuse his presence, but because he was trying to get down the step and into the alley, excuse me like he was trying to pass me on the sidewalk.

I rose slowly. His dark hair hung down over his face, skinny arms smudged in old tattoos like a sailor.

A love supreme, a love supreme.

I shifted under the weight of the guitar on my back. He lit a cigarette and stared up at what he could see of the sky through the leaves rippling in the sudden wind. I glanced up too, the clouds the conversation. He nodded and made to walk away.

But I turned up the volume on Coltrane and sped off again, before he could leave me, between steel fire escapes and clotheslines hanging heavy with towels.

true believers

There were parties at the band house where Thomas still lived. Now that Jude was with Lisa, and Henry had gone home, he'd invited the band Heavy Cheddar to move in with him—if the house was a disaster before, it was nothing compared to what Heavy Cheddar did to it. The walls were held up with beer cans and cigarette butts, broken guitars and wiry, ruined amps.

The night before Heavy Cheddar left for tour, the house was filled with celebratory chaos, and I was there, anonymous against the wallpaper, blind drunk with a bunch of people I only knew to look at. When I slipped out through the open front door to stand in the night and breathe fresh air, I hid by the bushes at the front of the house, nursing a drink that tasted like turpentine.

From behind me, yellow squares from the window threw themselves on the yard. Music thumped and squalled, there was hollering and wild laughter, crashes and shattering, as if people were throwing dishes at each other. A taxi pulled up on the front sidewalk, spilling girls from its interior, their laughter hard-edged as they tottered across the lawn with gappy little thighs, tight bellies flat above jutting hipbones. When the last person climbed from the car, I recognized his face and pushed myself further back into the shadows.

He paid the driver and sauntered up the sidewalk with a walk like Nick Cave, loping and long-legged. The girls had all gone inside, I could hear them stirring the pot with their sexual energy. I sucked on my smoke.

"Got a light?"

He stood in front of me but the shadows were so thick, he saw the spark of my cigarette first and my face after, when he came up close. "Nope," I said and as I passed him my cigarette, recognition flickered casually in his eyes. He opened his mouth to say something but a man in a mouse mask came from the house, one of the members of Heavy Cheddar.

"Sam, get in here. That magazine guy is here, he wants to talk to you. What are you...?" He didn't notice me until the last minute. "Oh sorry," he said, not sorry at all. His rubber whiskers quivering in the dusk. "Come on, man." And he grabbed Sam's arm, pulling him into the house.

Walking through the Plateau in the early morning, sky bloody and ravaged by early sun, clouds torn apart. Tall stone houses with windowsills heavy under red geraniums, trees meeting like hands above the street, leaves lush as new paint. It was only the beginning of the season but I was already exhausted.

When I turned the corner onto my street, Sam was standing outside my apartment. Smoking a cigarette and running his hands through his hair, smaller than I remembered. I strode up to him, preparing to tell him to get lost. My heart like a clenched fist. But before I could tell him, he threw down his cigarette and came close enough for me to smell sweat and tobacco, last night's sour beer.

"I heard about Ben," he said. "I never got to tell you I'm sorry."

My head bent awkwardly back against his shoulder. I squeezed my eyes shut against the sun. "Let's go inside," I finally said and we broke apart clearing our throats. Through the door to my apartment like we'd done it many times before and only my nerves told me it wasn't so.

My little room as he saw it must have seemed neglected. No one had come to my monastic mess since Jude used to teach me music on the red couch. Now the early sun stained the walls and I heard the echoes of old things. The guitar under its fog of dust. He took a seat on the edge of the couch.

"Do you want a drink?" I asked him, walking over to the kitchen, really just a sideboard with a sink and a stove and fridge. All I had was beer, a wilted head of lettuce, for some reason mustard.

When I turned back around, I was surprised afresh to see him on my couch, backlit by the window with its view of the street. He was like a hologram or a hallucination created solely by my desire. His skinny arms and legs jumbled and angular. "Here," I said, holding out a bottle. "How did you know where I live?" I didn't ask him why because I didn't want him to doubt his impulse to find me.

"I asked Thomas. I know you don't know me. But I wanted to make sure you were all right." He set his unopened drink on my coffee table and picked at the calluses on his fingertips with focus. "I know you probably have an idea of me inside your head because of all those stupid gigs."

"Why do you use the word stupid?" But there was something arrogant about the way he taunted women and danced about, loud and dark and careless.

"The band broke up."

"Seems to be a lot of that lately," I said.

When he spoke, he used his hands to accentuate his sentences, a conductor of conversation. In the revelation of natural light, I could see his bad skin, his yellowed teeth, the bags like bruises beneath his eyes. He was nothing more than an eidolon—I'd made too much of him. "It took two years to squeeze out one record. I don't know what the point was, I guess to have a relic. Who knows what will happen now. We're in our mid-thirties and not working toward anything tangible, it's all just a montage of bullshit and chaos. Scattered gigs. Drugs. House parties. I'm gonna come into my forties and have nothing but tall tales to show for my life. This isn't what being a musician was supposed to look like."

"What should it look like then?" I asked. I had no other pictures in my head.

"Music," he said. "I don't play my guitar unless we're having a jam, which only means doing drugs to the soundtrack of our own music."

I thought of Jude and his militant methodology. These days the word discipline shook me down.

"I did have an idea of you in my head," I told him. "But I'm glad you're different than that." I hated personas. I liked people the best when they were quiet and unwatched. At least I liked myself best that way. I moved toward him. But he stayed still.

When he spoke, he did not look at me. "I can't handle any emotional responsibility. If I have sex with you, then I'll be responsible for you."

I told myself at least he hadn't made me any promises. But I only had desire, instead of good sense. "I'm responsible for myself," I said.

"If we run into this with the same momentum that we've fucked up everything else, then all that'll be left is despair."

But I didn't want to believe in despair anymore—I was tired of keeping it near me just because I recognized its face.

And then we sat there, talked out of words. There came physical sensations after that, which arrived in a succession I could never undo.

Now I'm left to summary and soft-edged memories,
distorted from the space around them—but they're better
that way.

the makings of you

For the first time in my life I wanted the days to be predictable and sustainable instead of drunken stripes of light-
speed. The minutes so rich I could feel them slipping away
even before they happened. A memory before it began.

We had fallen into routine the way two people do—their
own pattern, like when pseudoscientists would praise water
molecules so that they would take a pretty shape. It was me
and him, and it looked like this: I woke up early and came
out to the living room, shutting the door behind me to let
him sleep. Sat on the red couch with a mug of instant coffee.
I picked up my acoustic guitar or wrote things down, silent
in the new sun. And then I'd go off into the day to run an
errand and come back to him making us eggs and toast. He
played guitar facing the wall while I read books or wrote
things down. In the middle of the day, I went off to whatever mindless job I happened to have at the time, and he
went back to his house, which I had never seen because we
were in that first sweet month, the world around us redacted
for our protection.

We puttered around in the evenings, windows open on
the purple summer air, the sound of children in the alleyway,
the cry of a lawnmower, the smell of charring meat. I wore

a white slip sitting on the edge of the sideboard and he told me again that he liked me, which made me proud of myself, as if I'd accomplished something just by letting him come around. Like, as opposed to love, was made up of all the tiny idiosyncratic shards of our personas. Like was how we got our hooks into each other, and it held all the respect and awe that familiar Love did not. That's what I told myself.

"What are you thinking?" he asked. Everyone always wanted to know what everyone else was thinking. As if our thoughts would mean anything to anyone else once we said them out loud.

"I guess I was seeing our bodies from the outside. I saw our bodies in bed and then out through the roof of the apartment and above the street into the trees, over the city until it broke through the sky."

He touched my skin, almost pinching me, reminding me there was an element of disbelief to everything we did, that we were dreaming. We were here and not here at all.

Sitting on my windowsill smoking cigarettes, fat candles sputtering beside us in the dark, we spied on the drunks stumbling over the cobblestone street. Nights like this only existed in seconds—Montreal wasn't a city, it was a perception glimpsed then lost again beneath soporific waves of wine.

Sam and I were wandering through Parc La Fountain over the pretty little bridge, holding hands and stretching our faces up at the late afternoon sun. Parc La Fountain where undulating white squirrels put their paws on their chests and said, *Who, me?* Where cyclists and old men and sunbathers and mothers with strollers met face to face on the paths, where the fountain spit up soapy water and ducks used the manmade lake as a toilet, where homeless men drowned and lay facedown for two weeks before police showed up to fish them out.

His friends waited impatiently on the hill, waving and shouting obscenities when they spotted us. Sam let go of my hand to wave back.

He introduced me as "my friend, Butterfly." In attendance was his roommate Monkey—I'd been told stories of him involving a threesome gone awry or a harrowing escape from a police officer at five in the morning. Monkey had bleached his hair and it had turned orange. He wore a striped shirt, striped socks, striped pants.

His girlfriend Mildred, strangled in a turtleneck, said to me, "Aren't you friends with that Pepper woman?" She had a way of staring down her nose as if performing aloof surgery.

Sam said, "She moved to Vancouver three months ago. Besides, no one is really friends with Pepper."

"Oh," sniffed Mildred.

I whispered to Sam, "Pepper moved away?"

"What does it matter?" he said. And I guessed it didn't.

With Mildred was a skinny girl with stringy black hair and brown lipstick. She said her name was Winifred and made a dramatic production of kissing me on the cheeks, only her lips connected with the air instead of my face. I think that's how she meant it. She kept bursting into tears unexpectedly, like when someone asked her how school was going.

Sam spread out a blanket in the patchy grass and someone brought out a few jugs of wine and a pack of smokes—it was a regular picnic.

Monkey talked about Mildred's last art show, where she'd stood naked in a bare white room cutting off her pubic hair with kitchen scissors yelling, "I am a woman! I am not a woman!"

"It was really cutting edge. Get it? Get it?" he said, elbowing Mildred in the ribs. She glared scathingly and blew cigarette smoke in his face. He fanned it away good-naturedly. "No, but actually it was great, a bunch of journalists came and everyone seemed angry and confused. I think you probably want that kind of reaction. Lots of arguing. And when we die we will be immortalized in a spray-painted mural on the side of a building downtown." ·

Winifred burst into tears, which made Sam jump. Glugging back purple wine, her teeth grey with it, she sobbed, "I need to pay my rent. I have to feed my dog! What is wrong with instant gratification?" Mildred gently took the wine bottle away.

Everyone else began yelling about money-making schemes and gender roles, sloshing wine, and rolling around on the blanket under the sun but I didn't have anything witty to say about making art or being a woman. Mildred put a hip-hop cassette into her portable tape player and cranked the sound. Monkey danced with her, something choreographed they must have practiced in their apartment living room.

Winifred shouted to be heard, trying to tell us about the history of inner-city rappers. She blubbered, "I know I'm not allowed to cry over their struggle because it's White Tears, but I just can't help it. I'm an empath."

Mildred finally threw herself against Sam, exhausted. He shrugged over at me. "I fucking have to eat right this second. And we have to go somewhere vegan OBVIOUSLY." She scowled pointedly at me. "Who are you again?" She left no space for an answer but hurriedly began gathering her effects. "Let's do this already," she snapped, yanking Monkey to his feet.

Sam turned to me. "You wanna come?"

"I can't..." I told him, and I don't even remember the excuse I used.

Sunday morning we walked along the overpass, yellow leaves scattered on the roofs of old warehouses painted with advertisements for products that hadn't existed since the thirties. Peeking over the concrete ledge down to the railroad tracks, I could see the pillars transformed into spray-painted masterpieces. White wine had a way of alchemizing your spirit into a shape with no corners or edges. A wine hangover was all of that plus a headache. I gazed at everything mistily—like how they'd shoot old film stars with a soft lens when they'd beg their lovers not to leave.

"Where are we going?" I asked Sam as we headed down through the streets, the lipstick-red leaves making noises like hushing mothers when we rushed through them. Over Sherbrooke with its hailstorm of cars, the air smelling of coffee, oranges, cold showers, toast. We went downtown, where the alleys were black and greasy, slimy and full of trash, unlike the alleys of the Plateau with its pretty lanes full of cats and flowers.

We stopped somewhere and got cigarettes. And then arrived in Griffintown. "Enjoy this while you can," Sam said when I stopped to examine an old factory. He spit on the sidewalk. "In a year this will all be condos and fancy charcuterie shops. This whole place is going to be overrun with yuppies. Family means nothing to real estate cyborgs." He'd grown up in Griffintown with his grandmother. "My mother wanted to take me to Paris with her when she left. She said this neighbourhood was a ghetto. But everything I am is in the wreck of these little industrial streets."

"Hey! You two!" A man with long permed hair, dyed black, a top hat and sunglasses, came clattering up beside us in one of those horse-and-carriage contraptions the tourists were fond of. The driver smoked a cigarette with stained yellowed fingers and waved us over. "Get in sweethearts, get in. My horse has the shits so I'm takin' her back to the stables. You want a free ride in my romantic carriage? You're a cute couple."

"Why not? We gotta go that way anyway," Sam said.

We climbed up into the wooden carriage painted the colour of dirty bubblegum, faded fake flowers wound along the frame. The driver began telling us all about his obsession with Guns and Roses and how he'd gone to see them in Toronto. He told us his horse's name was Axl.

"This neighbourhood is doomed," he said. "Doomed. They're going to level it. It will be unrecognizable." The horse kept farting, terrible smells puncturing the air. "Mary!" The man hollered. "Mary, we need you! Drive these real estate vampires out of here so we can be left in peace! This is not our way! This isn't Toronto. Send them to Vancouver. Calgary. Edmonton!" He pretended to barf as we clopped along.

I mouthed at Sam, "Who's Mary?" Thinking he was referring to the virgin.

"The headless hooker," he whispered back. "Mary Gallagher comes to Williams Street every seven years or so, searching for her head. Used to scare the shit out of me as a kid. I thought she'd wanna come get her revenge on me because I was happy in the same place where she'd been killed."

It started raining, one of those light morning drizzles that made you want to go straight back to bed even if it was only nine in the morning.

I was surprised to hear Sam say he'd had a happy child-hood. He'd told me his time with his grandmother hadn't ended well. She'd gotten ovarian cancer and when his mother had to come back from Paris to take care of him, she returned with an unexpected husband. His grandmother went to the hospital and never left. His mother and the new husband had moved Sam out to a farmhouse in the Eastern Townships. He'd been thirteen. He'd told me all about the farmhouse and when I said it sounded beautiful, he'd said "Sure. A beautiful prison."

"Last stop, lovebirds," our driver hollered, pulling up at the Horse Palace. He should have been on a stage some-where. Instead he was loose on the streets with a worn-out gassy horse who shit into a black bag tied to its ass.

The sagging wood-plank stables were alive with the smell

of horse—it hit me full in the face as we rolled in. "Thanks for the lift," Sam said, taking my hand and leading me through the lot. On the periphery of the neighbourhood we could see the rising condos like an an oncoming chemical spill.

"My whole family was born here—my grandmother, my great grandmother. My great grandfather worked on the canal when they came from the Ukraine. He wouldn't recognize this stupid place now," he said. "They've put a highway through his backyard. They're defacing our heritage with concrete and plate glass. These condos are a fucking infection. Fuck." He took my hand, pulling me toward a narrow brick building. "Come on, we can go in here."

The rain started coming down in sheets, dumping on our shoulders like an upturned bucket. I stopped him. The way his hair was slicked back in the rain, the way it spiked his eyelashes, the way he stood there helpless in his ruined neighbourhood, something inside me fell to its knees. The running water on our faces made our lips slippery. We kissed in the way that you only can when everything is going to shit.

When we got inside I began to shiver. "Get out of your clothes," he said, unbuttoning my shirt. He undressed me and then yanked off his shirt, tripping out of his pants and leaving our stuff in a sodden pile in the corner.

To get into the building he'd picked a key out of the fistful he wore clipped to his hip. "I've got the only key now," he'd said. "The place still rightfully belongs to Anna. They couldn't get her to sell it. She left it to me in her will." Anna, his grandmother. "I gotta figure out how the fuck to pay property tax or something. I don't know how anything works."

The place was one big echoing open space full of cobwebs, but the wooden floors still gleamed beneath the grime. The windows climbed all the way to the ceiling. A dance barre ran the length of the brick wall. "I could make a fortune selling it to some real estate conglomerate. Everyone wanted me to turn it into a venue or have parties or something, but I cannot for the life of me picture people in here puking on the floor, pissing in the corners, having sex upstairs. No thanks. All that paperwork to turn it into what? Another gentrified pile of crap like all these other new-wave barber and charcuterie shops? Specialty meatball joints and gin pubs? Give me a fucking break."

A flaking piano sat in the corner with yellowed ivory keys, an acoustic guitar leaning against its side. The only other piece of furniture was a washed-out wardrobe. He flung open its doors and a cloud of moths flew out like scraps of cotton. "Dammit," he said, pushing aside hanging tutus. "I forgot about mothballs." The tutus were not pink but long gauzy things the colour of skin in a Degas painting—I could see him smoking and sketching from a corner.

Sam grabbed two dresses, one soft and white—he gave that to me and put on the other dress, some ripped black lace thing, his wet hair dripping onto his shoulders left droplets across the yellow floor. I wanted to remember us always like this, wearing an old woman's dresses and tiptoeing through an abandoned building.

"When I lived here with Anna I used to hide upstairs and watch her teach dance class. The ballerinas were so graceful. If I came down they wanted to kiss my cheeks over and over so I stayed upstairs." I laughed, picturing him rubbing his eyes in one-piece pajamas, bony dancers kissing his tiny face like birds pecking the water. He picked up our wet clothes and hung them on a banister that wound like black ribbon up the length of the brick wall. If our memories had a sound it would be the noise of our echoing feet.

The upstairs had a mezzanine overlooking the floor below. It was so far down it made my knees sing. By the far window was a little kitchen, black and white tiles, cupboards with chipped green paint. To the right of the kitchen stood two doors. He beckoned me with a finger. I would follow those fingers anywhere.

I had a chance to peek in the first door as we walked past. I spied empty dress racks and peeling butterfly wallpaper— the butterflies had flown free of the walls, leaving behind faded empty paper. I could see Anna sitting in front of a white vanity with lightbulbs around the mirror, studying the reflection of her elegant face.

I imagined them walking along the canal in the autumn under flaming trees, Anna in a white fur coat and Sam dressed in a sailor suit holding onto her hand. When he got older she gave him his first guitar and he'd go down to the water alone picking away at it until night came.

His bedroom had been left behind. He told me that when Anna had to go into the hospital they'd sold all her beautiful things, the chandeliers and the vanity, the canopy bed and the mirrors with golden frames. All of it went to antique stores on rue Notre Dame. But Sam's bedroom had been passed over as if he'd painted blood above the door-frame. His childhood dreams hadn't been worth hawking, you couldn't get a hundred bucks for his memories. Sam's little bedroom had a red-and-blue hammock hung in the corner beside a bookshelf cluttered like a pile of leaves. His bed against the opposite wall with a blanket printed in a pattern of stars, the big dipper, the little dipper, the constellations of Leo and Pisces.

"I should have gotten rid of this shit," he said, seeing everything through my eyes. "But everyone was so quick to get rid of everything. I wanted some proof to say I was there, that this happened to me."

I had a dream we were walking on a dark road through the country, the night illuminated by orange highway lights.

The screaming wind kept getting stronger and stronger until it felt as if my arms were going to be ripped from their sockets. A hurricane coming straight for us. And then it was above us. I could see up inside it right into the cyclical eye. We were going to be blown off our feet. We needed to take shelter inside a claw-foot tub or kneel on a rubber-backed bathmat so when the lightning struck us we wouldn't get electrocuted. We ran to an abandoned barn on the side of the road and crouched behind the skeletal frame of wood. But still the sky raged and came for us.

living with the black dog

Sitting on Sam's lap on the café terrace under the yellow umbrellas, wearing his sweater big as a blanket. We were quiet before we drank our coffee. And after, when I felt too small for my skin, he said, "I have to tell you something." He kept pinching the cigarette between his fingers.

A cold silvery feeling went through my esophagus like mercury in a thermometer. I remembered Thomas' phone call, to tell me Ben had died. I wrapped his sweater tightly around me. I got up and sat in another chair so I could see his face when he said it.

"I'm going to L.A."

There. "L.A. Ha. Of course you're going to L.A. We're all going to L.A."

"I'm serious, B," he said and I saw him new and again, the face I knew sleeping, the promises he never made.

I stole his cigarette and watched the cars curse each other in the narrow one-way street. Now what would I do with the afternoon? "I'm happy for you. That's good news for you, right?"

"It is good news. For me."

"Fuck sakes," I said, exhaling smoke up into the umbrella. It hovered like a storm. I was suddenly tired but I would have to keep going.

"I'm not leaving for a few weeks. We have time."

"Time for what?"

"For whatever it is we're doing."

I stood and stretched my arms over my head. "What are we doing?"

He wanted to touch me, but didn't. Instead he stood up too, threw his cigarette butt into the road. "I have to take off. I gotta go pick up my visa today."

"No kidding."

He ran his hand through my hair, messing it up, gulped down the last of his coffee, glancing restlessly up and down St. Laurent Boulevard, shiny with morning. "I can't believe I'm leaving Montreal. I will be fucked up in another city. My charms will be lost." He was trying to smile, waiting for me to tell him he was loved and that everything would be fine.

"See you later," I said. I felt the need to go for a brisk walk, to do mundane things to keep me on the ground, to pull me back out of the meteor shower that had been my time with Sam. We could have not met at all. I could have been somewhere else and he could have been somewhere else. There could be a hundred parallel universes where we'd had babies or had never been born at all.

And just like that he was off to finish the plans I never knew about until I got close enough he felt he had to tell me. I watched the lope of his walk, movements I had imprinted in my databank of recognized gestures. I thought of his long fingers. I scanned the holograph I had of him in my head to make sure it was safely detailed there for when it would be all I'd have.

free your mind and your ass will follow

Sometimes when I went out at night I could see old age on everyone's faces, the threat of lines and falling structure. But I was immortal in these days. I couldn't imagine living a life that was less spontaneous, less unpredictable, less infinite.

Down the street in a daze, I found myself in the dépanneur staring blankly at cat food. The man behind the counter with an enormous moustache had his children working the cash register, all of them smiling and not caring that it was hot outside or that the entire store smelled of rotting cardboard. The place sold door chimes and long distance phone cards, red and gold paper horses faded from the sun, dusty cans of beans, cheap wine and forties of beer that tasted like nails. The floor layered in black plastic runways and littered with bags of potato chips, wasabi peas, expired deodorant, all of it half in boxes, half out. A tiny television in the corner turned to the channel with the soap operas.

I wandered from aisle to aisle studying the expiry dates on packaged rice.

"Psst," I heard, and jerked my head around. There was Thomas, stuffing shit into his pockets like his apartment was on fire. Whistling and winking, he grabbed my arm and dragged me out of the place behind him, cackling like a fool.

"That was subtle," I snapped as we ducked down the alleyway. "Why don't you take your klepto ways to the Wal-Mart, you little punk? That man in there probably collects empty cans on his days off."

"Relax," he said, unwilling to back down. "If corporations are allowed to enslave us then I should be able to five finger a pastry from the dépanneur."

"Oh wow. Nice speech. Real eloquent."

"Why are you being such an asshole?" Thomas asked, wide-eyed.

I squinted up at the buzzing sun. "Sam's leaving."

"He's moving away? Is he going to come back?" Thomas tugged on my arm to get me walking up the narrow alley, kicking at garbage and scaring stray cats with our noise.

"How should I know? I only found out an hour ago. I don't know when I'll see him again. We had good times." I jumped to grab a skinny tree branch over my head, yanking it loose with a snapping sound.

"Maybe you can visit him."

"Oh sure." But I had no idea how I would become someone who could afford an international flight. I guessed people did it all the time, worked a job, saved up money, got on a plane. I analyzed my own life but lost the plot immediately. It was easier to sit with the familiar and let everyone else move around me. I said, "Let's go drink a beer somewhere while it's still summer."

A few hours later, we were heavy with beer and sun. The streets full of people. Everything was its brightest colour. I couldn't imagine it being white and dead again, frigid and fast asleep, the icy core of January in Montreal.

Thomas and I walked arm in arm through the street, steam erupting from the restaurant backs and stray cats racing past, tourists jostling around us. We headed up toward the sprawling park where old men slouched on benches and sinister angel statues reached for the sky.

Into the trees, climbing over boulders and winding around ashy abandoned fire pits, deep in the mountain park. Thomas huffed and puffed, "Hup, two, three, four!"

We didn't see anyone else. I kept expecting woodland creatures to come poking around the bushes but this was the city. The squirrels were pimps and thieves and the deer had disappeared. From behind the leaves the traffic roared invisibly. As we came over the rise, hiking up the narrow path, we saw a policeman standing under the trees.

"What's he doing up here?" Thomas whispered. The man guarded a yellow tarp on the ground, bulky with its cargo. A grey hand sticking out. We had to walk past the officer to continue up the path. He gave us a nod but kept staring straight ahead.

"Is there a dead person under there?" I said.

He looked at me sharply, eyes the colour of metal. In his Quebecois English he said, "He was a runner had a heart attack. I wait for paramedics."

We went on. When we reached the top of the royal mountain it was flooded with tourists and kids in sleek cars blasting terrible club music. They stared as we walked past. I thought about the silent corpse lying under the trees, the grey hand.

And there was our city laid out like a tiny pastel movie set beneath the sky. Thomas pointed out buildings and land-marks. "There's Brooms. There's the house. There's the old jam space."

The sun began its descent behind buildings and bridges. How reluctantly it went. I wondered if we'd be like that when our time came, hanging on saying, "Five more minutes." But then I thought about Ben and how quickly his life came and went. The runner on the mountain probably expected to be home for dinner by now.

"Let's go," I said, when all we could see was a fingernail clipping of the sun. We picked our way slowly down the darkening trail when suddenly the bushes alighted with the blinking inhale-exhale flash of fireflies. I tried to remember the last time I'd seen fireflies and called to mind a vague memory of holding out tiny hands with a glass jar, the sprinkle of lights landing on my fingertips.

"I think every kid has a memory of fireflies, whether it's real or not," Thomas said, somewhere beside me in the dark. He took my arm because it was hard to see and we made our way down the little mountain, back into the warm city still holding leftovers of the sun—orange-black shadows wrapping around us like a long goodbye.

lonely richard

His songs matched my insides, and here was this sudden person sculpting images out of sounds, stepping on peddles to bring forward lights and blinking cities, scarves of phosphorescence through the air like electric snow.

I drank wine with Sam in his bedroom, at his house at last, his friends running up and down the stairs, and us sequestered behind the closed door.

When I opened my eyes again, the sheets were cold and the bed was empty. I pressed the creaking door open and crept down the dark hall, strange rooms opening up against it. And then I heard music and came into the living room. Sitting on the carpet surrounded by short sputtering candles sat Sam in a circle of people—some of them must have lived in the house, but the rest of them were unknown to me. He was playing *Chelsea Hotel No. 2* by Leonard Cohen. It dawned on me that I had never really heard that song until that night.

In the last days, time yanked itself out from under us like a failed magic trick and the last night came smashing. Loving

114

someone was like discovering a beautiful song for the first time: you couldn't stop listening to it in an attempt to figure out why it did what it did to you until you were fooled into thinking the song was your own.

Ricochet Bonanza had a last gig at Brooms on the night before he left Montreal. His band nearly destroyed the venue. People went mad, thrashing all over the place, wasted blind in tribute. His band members were animals. Girls wept openly. The bar tender kept bringing over platters of shots.

He caught my eye from across the room, long looks full of meaning before sticking out his tongue. Our lives were just a series of hi's and bye's. I thought the day would arrive with fire and brimstone, Miles Davis playing trumpet in the sky. But it came as quietly as all the other unmarked days.

I drank more than I'd meant to. I had wanted to stay sharp and preserve the experience but it blurred out from under me. I surrendered, drunk and defeated.

We didn't get back to his apartment until four in the morning, only two short hours left to us. I guess I shed a tear when my face was hidden in his neck, the shameful sentimental tears of a drunk. I thought he wouldn't notice but he said, "B, you crying?" I floated above us in a near-death experience. And before I could barter with the clock for five more minutes of grace his alarm shattered the silence. He jumped up and switched on the lamp, hopping around the room with one leg in his pants and one leg out, an unlit smoke in the corner of his mouth.

I sat there rubbing my tired eyes, the taxi honking from the street.

Sam lifted me up into his arms. He said, "I love you, I love you, I love you," stumbling and spinning me in circles and it was supposed to mean something.

Then we were out on the sidewalk, the driver throwing his bags into the trunk with no emotion. He had seen a thousand taxi cab partings and was no longer affected by any of them.

Sam tucked himself inside the backseat of the car, his long legs folded up like an umbrella. He reached for my hand through the rolled down window but the driver pulled impatiently into the street.

"Goodbye!" Sam called from the window of the car.

"Goodbye!" I yelled back, but my words were lost in the reverb of the city.

Staying in touch with Sam after he left was like trying to yell across the Grand Canyon. To fill the gaps of loneliness I put on a brave face and went running through the daily routines. His friends, every time they heard his holy name, gushed the same lines like they'd practiced them in private: "We're so thrilled for him. *Good* for him." Their enthusiasm was irritating but it was I who had clasped my hands around him too tightly and held on.

dream in A Minor

At any moment I expected the ground to shake or the sidewalk to split, anything to prove I was alive, anything to prove this wasn't a dream. Anything to wake me up.

It catches between my lips, a vice around my throat, a choke of breath. Chilly morning wind tiptoeing across my bare arms, raising the hairs. The bedroom window left open overnight and the white curtain swelling like laundry on a line. I stretch out my arm beside me and feel the empty space of the other side of the bed. The cool wood of the floor beneath my feet.

I'm a ghost in my own house. The quiet like two soft hands cupped around my ears and they throb with it. I pad down the hallway and into the kitchen below. The open space is full of air, its white walls, windows with a view of the trees. You can barely see the road, it's like being in a tree house in the Los Angeles canyon. I slide open the balcony door and step into the morning sun, the wood warm under my feet. I lean against the railing and close my eyes. There is no evidence he was ever here at all.

There had been a series of smouldering heatwaves, wasps fucked up from cellphones droning woozily around, birds singing their sun-tired songs from somewhere far off. The buzz of cicadas, heat rippling across the road.

Leaning over the balcony railing to ash our cigarettes, he used to run his grainy fingertips down over me. The fat black road running down the hill in a ribbon of warm tar to the grid-lock of the city, steel and cement and noise. I faced the leaves. No one heard us up here, our pleasure. We sat in the same chair in the middle of the day. I guess that was the dream.

The truck stalls twice under my hand, keys and heartbeat, then the dirt clears its throat under the tires and I rip out of the driveway, down the snake-shaped road. I take the corners like I want another head-on collision and reach the six lanes before I'm ready, flashing sun on steel, the noise, the trash of it.

Blindly I somehow take myself where I think I should go, down the canyon road onto the boulevard where the sun goes down. The wide street lined with palm trees, skinny directionless birds. The sky bleached colourless.

I drive as blindly as everyone else until I get to the road with The Jam Space, a bar by the little stone bridge. Across the way from Hard Times Pizza, which had gotten us through a lot of those. Everything buzzes in the ugliness of the sun.

The Jam Space is a wreck of a building, the structure perilous, the sign hand-painted in cocaine scrawl. You wouldn't know it was there if you didn't know what you were looking for. I park the truck and go round back, past the dumpster, and climb the warped steps hanging onto the pipe railing in case the stairs fall out from under me. Music pounds against the black-painted windowpanes, even now in the washed out haze of the morning.

I pull open the metal door. The darkness and the stench of sour beer shove me back for a minute until I adjust. The hallway painted red like the inside of an esophagus. Smashed mirror mosaics and band posters half-hanging everywhere line the walls. The esophagus opens up into the belly of the bar, its central feature a sloping stage. A few haggard long-hairs squint out at me from under the muddy sound—they're the Friday night session players gone on into Saturday morning. Eric, Jonas, Will.

Have you seen Rev? I shout up over the noise.

They give me that blank musician stare, the expression you get when you try to interrupt mid-jam. They watch me for a minute then finish up their conversation, screeching guitar, hammering bass, insistent percussion.

You looking for someone? Eric puts down his blistered instrument and sits on the lip of the stage, eye-level with me. He would look twenty-five if he ever got some sleep. He's in a hooded sweatshirt.

I pull my fingers through my hair, unbrushed for days. I was wondering if you knew where Rev went, I say. I woke up this morning and he was gone.

Why do you think we'd know where this person is? Will lifts his head from where he had been tuning his guitar with concentration.

What do you mean? My fingers clench the edge of the stage, the painted plywood tacky under my hands.

I guess I mean, Will says, why do you think we'd know *who* this person is?

Funny. That's a good one, fucking hilarious.

They exchange uneasy glances like I've taken too much. Jonas stretched his arms over his head, cracks his knuckles. I think you're mixed up, sweetheart, he calls to me from across the top of his sprawling kit. The other two turn back to their amps, cranking up the volume so that the feedback screams into my face with violence and I'm washed away in a wall of sound.

Every person I saw was a mirage. I trudged over the pavement trying not to scream at the sky. It had been, or was supposed to be, a huge experience, but I felt my smallness sharpened against the sun, I was an ant burning up under a magnifying glass.

The definition of one particular word is *mind-manifesting*, but my manifestations weren't limited to my mind. Because I remember him there, when he told me he'd been sick and tired and defeated, but you wouldn't have known it from the way he played his guitar. If he was the sidewalk, his songs were the green things coming out of the cracks.

After I leave The Jam Space all I can do is drive. I drive on every single street and stop for gas three times. The city full of blinding light. I drive past tiny bungalows that look like magic dollhouses, little white houses with orange roofs, steel gates that fence in the front yards. San Pedro cacti crowd together in clay pots like gangs of aliens. I drive under towering palms that dapple spiky sunshine onto the roads. And somehow wind up on the boulevard that looks out over the Pacific, canals and tiny shops and gentle streets, my favourite neighbourhood. I park the truck and step out into the day.

I walk over to the music store. Rev loved this place. He'd stand around for hours with his eyes upturned to worship the wall of guitars, everything gleaming in reds and greens and blues, the colour of jewels.

The patrons in the store never change. There's the childish prodigy showing off on the piano. The metal-head with pubic-hair goatee shredding on a Flying V. Some garage-rocking dad playing Stairway to Heaven.

The store is full of cables and gadgets and gear, a great and beautiful machine. The front counter loaded down with containers of guitar picks bright as fish. I elbow my way up to the counter where a cashier pretends to sleep against a stack of music books.

Have you seen Rev this morning?

He gives me a slow blink like a turtle. Is that somebody who works here? he asks. I've only been here a week, so… He glances down at his nametag as if he's still learning what it means.

No, he doesn't *work* here. You know us, we're always in here. We're in here almost every day. But he's shaking his head at me like an idiot. I can hear the rising blood in my ears. I feel like I'm trying to talk underwater. You sold us guitar strings yesterday. It was *you* who rang us in!

His eyes dart over my shoulder to the growing line of customers. He wields his pricing gun for protection, his voice cracking as he says, I honestly have no clue what you're talking about.

The last thing I remember is grabbing the plastic bowl of guitar picks and throwing them across the room.

The sky the colour of an old bruise, poison clouds came down in trails. There was no music. Everything was built of bones, I was born inside a skeleton. Drifting like a seed, I flew into the face of the sun, where things lived that couldn't survive without light. That was a onetime dream. We were moving toward the canyon house on a highway of handwritten words, manifestos, our little prayers.

Almost every night you could go down into the city and find him somewhere, hidden behind his hair, deep in a wall of song. I got drawn in—it was impossible not to.

When the sun goes down I head for home, alone. The day hangs on my shoulders like a cross. I drive slowly up the hill, back to the house inexplicably empty. I flip on a light but it only makes the house look darker. He's still not here.

I go upstairs, climb into the white sheets with my shoes on and close my eyes. Which is how he went away in the first place.

I go to the market and a lizard rings me in at the register, its acid green face grinning. Grapefruits turn into baby faces, pink and pulpy. The floor tiles become pyramid tiers and for a minute you were almost beside me as I ran up the side of the tower but when I try to touch you, you turn into a column of smoke and blow away across the sky.

There's perfect mastery in the lines on your hands, a camaraderie with your veins, the hidden secrets of your blueprint body. Underneath my exterior is a grid of guitar wire criss-crossed and ricocheting electric light. Inside the massive bleeding heart, heavy warm lonely sad and screaming love.

In a clash of trash can lids and sudden light two raccoons streak through the empty lot. Under the mist, past the busted-up swing set where two people rock back and forth, stoned in their drooping swings, hidden behind smoke and quiet talk. But then the mist clears and there is only one person on the swings. Swinging fast, head thrown back, feet at the stars, eyes closed on the night.

I find a squirrel tail on the sidewalk. A crushed butterfly in the grass. What is that song, what is that sound, where was it born? Keep walking, just to walk, just to be alive.

There was life outside us, but it went on with or without us. I traced my fingers along the circumference and found arches and doorways that crumbled into crazy worlds. The way we played got into our bones.

You've come in here every night looking for that man. Clearly, he does not want to be found, the bartender says, slouching over the wooden bar top sour from spilled beer.

Maybe you're wrong.

What's your name?

B, I tell her. My hands on the bar like white mice skirting the edge of a trap. He played guitar. Everyone around here knew him.

Well I don't and I've been working here for five years. I know every musician that comes around. You some sort of groupie?

Sure, I said.

Your invisible man with the guitar sounds like nothing but a pretty little story, she said. But she was pouring me a shot as she spoke. Listen, I'm sorry. You should come down here and play some of your own music. She leans on her elbow, black eyes in a raven face. She is probably a bike courier by day with that DIY haircut, there are feathers inked along her arms. Her head cocked sideways like she's looking for something shiny.

It can get weird up in the woods. I pace the wooden floor, feeling the soft cool grain. The hours are long and short. Silence has a way of washing over you, dragging you out until all you can see is the sun and a long blue line of sea. I touch my guitar and the strings echo tunelessly around the room, swallowed up by the walls of silence. How long has it been? A week? A month? How long had he been here for? Infinity? Never? I go back to pacing the floors.

Coming back to the house is like returning from a war—nothing is recognizable. The more beautiful the house is, the uglier it becomes. Grey clouds opaque as wool engulf me and drag me out of bed, pulling on my arms so they're stretched in the shape of a Vitruvian Man.

I'm swept across the expanse of the sprawling city until my feet touch bottom on the sidewalk of the boulevard. The sky flashes with flits of lightening and I duck into a record store to get out of the sudden rain. The smell of dusty cardboard and vinyl is as familiar as the smell of my own skin. My fingers tripping across the record tops as easy as writing my name.

The walls of the narrow store are painted black, cracked disks nailed up like photographs. The clerk in her checked shirt and plastic glasses has her face buried in a music magazine and whatever is coming from the record player is so familiar that I hum along on instinct. I know that song. He wrote it. My head comes up like a listening deer.

The door at the back of the shop, going into the alley, slams suddenly and I catch a glimpse of his fingers. I would recognize that hand in a crowd of a thousand people. The record I'm holding falls to the floor and smashes into three jagged pieces as I run after him.

The clerk hollers but I'm already going down the fire-escape and jumping down to the pavement, startling a mangy cat as it picks its way around the trash. I run out into the street. I can hear the song louder now like it crept from my ears and into the air, bouncing off buildings, it rocks the parked cars.

The clouds split themselves with electricity. I smash past people, running up the street where he vanished into the crowd. I run from the boulevard and hit Vin Scully Avenue, creep over the rise of Lilac Place and as soon as I get into Elysian Park the clouds tear open as if by a pair of massive hands.

I go in under the trees, head along the narrow path, the pavement baked flat and black as a tar cake. The rain rises steam up from the hot earth and there's the smell of water hitting pavement. I duck further in under the lace of the trees and sit with my back against a trunk, listening to rain dancing on the tops of cars. Pulling my cold legs up under my chin and closing my eyes, the lonely sounds pull me away with them.

When I wake up, dawn has come and gone, I can tell by the colour of the sky. My legs are stiff as old wires. I stretch them out in front of me in the dirt, cracking my knees, rubbing my eyes. The air is full of morning smells, fresh wind not yet dirtied by the city. When we used to wake up this early we'd go get coffee, huddling together at a wrought iron table in the fog, smoking cigarettes and telling each other our weird dreams.

I walk down out of the park and see the truck parked there. I have no memory of parking it but the keys are in the pocket of my jeans. The inside of the truck is already getting hot as the sun pulls itself from the horizon. I drive onto the road, still rubbing at my eyes to get the haze out.

Jesus, you wanna slow down a bit? a voice comes from the backseat.

I think I shout something as I pull the truck over, tires squealing. A hundred drivers lean on their horns as they tear past. I whip around in my seat, tangled in my seatbelt. Sitting there natural as if I was her taxi is the girl from the record store. She's still wearing the checked shirt and big plastic glasses, now a smile full of teeth.

The fuck are you doing in my truck?

You owe me a record.

How did you even get in here?

I'm going to need you to give me some cash. You dropped Prince's Black Album.

That's insane. No I didn't.

She shrugs. Ah, maybe it was just the Beatles. I don't remember. And yet here I am. Please pay me now. She's gesturing at my glove compartment.

I give her a look but automatically click open the glove compartment anyway, find a crumpled twenty. Here. Hope it's enough.

Thank *youuuuu*, she drawls, tucking it away. You wanna go get a coffee then? My treat.

Gee, thanks. I pull back out onto the road.

You're in the record store a lot, you and that man, she says conversationally.

I almost hit the car in front of me. So you've seen me before. You've seen the person I was with then. I peek back at her in the rearview mirror.

She's biting her fingernail and studying it. Sure I've seen you and him. I see everyone who come into the store, I'm not blind. You guys are regulars.

I pull in at the first coffee place I see.

We were standing at the foot of the bed in the white bedroom, watching the night creep away across the tops of the trees, the orange light pollution of the city melting in after it. The window open, curtain dancing in the wind.

A white butterfly flew in through the window and landed on the headboard. Another one landed on the floor. A few more followed, up on the curtain rod, flickering their ragged wings. And then they all came, every single white butterfly in the city, through the window like a storm. They beat a wind against our cheeks and fluttered around our heads. They covered our bed like a field of moving flowers, they flew through the air like a heavy snow, they blotted out the dawn, they crowded the air like the aftermath of a pillow fight.

I raised my hands above my head and they flew in between my fingers. I spun in a circle and they wound around me like ribbons. They landed on my eyelids, their dusty wings pulsing against the sides of my head until the room was too full to move.

She's tucked up in the brown plastic booth at The 101 Coffee Shop as if she was born there. It's as if her casual mention of him back in the truck is as invisible as the man himself. She's not saying shit.

I trace my finger over the brown-and-blue mosaic wall and imagine old gumshoes meeting dames here to solve the mystery of their missing lovers. My coffee matches my thoughts. I finally bring it up.

That man you said you saw me with…

Yes? Her eyes are far too intense to meet for more than five seconds at a time.

Have you seen him since?

Nope. Haven't you?

I drain my coffee. No. He's gone. And I don't know where. You're the only one who's even acknowledged his existence. Even his old bandmates don't know where he's gone. To myself, I think, they don't even know he exists.

I've always been able to see things others can't, ever since I was a kid. You know, like ghosts or auras. Yours is white, by the way. She grabs my hand and examines my torn up fingertips like a jeweller looking over stones. Do you play guitar?

I retract my hand. Kind of. I want to know about my white aura, I want to tell her that he isn't a ghost. I want to stay in this part of the conversation but she's already moved along.

You play enough to wear your fingers down. And then she starts chattering about music and how she plays bass or something, but I can't grab a word to hang onto.

He is a subliminal message in a movie flickering between the frames. He is an SOS telegram tapped against my temple. He beats beneath the words like a second heart.

Wanna come? she's asking and I try to retrace the conversation to know what she's talking about but I've lost track.

I examine her long thin hair, plaid shirt, her bold grey eyes. Maybe that's where her name came from; she told me back in the truck that she was called Grey. She could be anybody going anywhere. And like a door opening inside me, I realize I could also be that free.

Sure, I say. Why not.

We walk into The Jam Space like we're walking into a tiger's den. I read somewhere that tigers eat women because of their pheromones. I stick close to the side of my new friend. The place is packed and I don't recognize anyone—the red lights distort everything like a liquid heart.

The bike courier is behind the bar again. I realize that in all the times I'd come here with Rev, I had never seen her. Whipping around glinting bottles like revolvers, laughter about her like a murder of crows. When she sees me, she winks. The band onstage is some funk trio trying to be the next Red Hot Chilli Peppers, only none of them can play their instruments.

I spot The Jam Space's owner, an old bluesman in a tropical shirt. He's making slashing motions at his throat and pointing at the stage.

Give the kids a laptop computer and suddenly every one of 'em thinks they're a goddamn artist, he says. Pours himself a shot of gin and throws it back.

Grey pulls me over to the bar. The bike courier is suddenly nowhere to be found and someone else serves us beers. The band is making clever noise, screaming feedback. My ears ache. They finish their set to scattered pockets of applause and I turn, yelling *Thank God* to Grey but now she's gone too.

I scan the dark room and find her stomping onto the stage. She shoos the band off and snatches one of their guitars. I need this, I see her mouthing to the scrawny kid. He flees.

Grey slings the guitar across her body and says into the microphone, Hope you don't mind, but I think we need a change of pace. And then she starts strumming the guitar as hard as she can. She plays five songs in a row, songs that sound the same as she looks, skinny and raw and full of booze. She screams, Bring back the bees and butterflies!

The bed I wake up in doesn't belong to me. I don't recognize the smells. Beside me is the bike courier with her DIY haircut. Her eyes still closed. The sun peeks through the window with a bloodshot eye then disappears again. I pull my bones upright and tiptoe across the room to the window. I think I'm in Venice Beach. I hold my breath while I gather my clothes off the carpet and slip through the door.

Nothing is dark as the canyon at night. The last of the city animals wail from the trees until the morning light returns and they see it was only their imaginations.

My eyes as wide as they will go take in shapes on the highway, the darkness a seeping and sinister fog. I'd spent the day at Grey's apartment, sprawled on her deep carpet in her bedroom, listening to records all day. We smoked joints and drank hot chocolate and didn't talk.

Now the headlights of the truck squint through the night and make me feel like a robber as I crawl through the hills. I can almost see the dirty white letters strung across the hill. I can almost see real stars.

We turn our eyes upward as if we can force success to take a tangible shape just by looking in the right direction.

I'm in the bike courier's bed again, Nedra is her name. Washed up on the beach of some random morning. She slips out of bed.

Coffee? she asks but she's already sashaying into the kitchen. I can hear her rattling around. My mouth tastes like pennies. I pull the white sheet over my head and stare at my body, a pile of pale appendages. It can respond to anything, it can do anything, it can belong to anyone. But not to me.

When I walk through my front door Grey is sitting cross-legged right in the middle of the kitchen tabletop. She has a dark purple bass laying beside her.

Welcome home, she says sarcastically. She's smoking a cigarette, ashing on her jeans and rubbing it into the fabric. The sun comes fat and lazy through the window. What did you think of my performance the other night anyway? I forgot to ask. She hops off the table, chucks her cigarette butt in the sink, and starts rifling through my cupboards like a raccoon.

I wonder what Rev would have thought about Grey and I going through the unmarked hours with no plans or structures. He never slept in anymore. He left that back in Montreal with the drugs and the bad weather. He'd be shut up in a room somewhere, studying theory and going over scales.

Your performance?

Yeah, you probably don't remember. Someone kept feeding you whiskey.

Her name is Nedra.

Whatever. Listen, I've given it some thought. She hops up on the counter with a mouth full of cereal, using a pot instead of a bowl. I've given it some thought, she says again as if she is still giving it some thought, and I've decided I'm going to let you join my band.

I fill up the teapot and chuck it on the stove. What band?
I talked to that bartender, your little pal Nedra with the
bad haircut. She says we can have a slot at The Jam Space
whenever we want.

The tea kettle starts screaming and I burn my hand on
the steam. Well then, I say.

The canyon house is two levels, one big open space for
the living room and kitchen, and one big open space for
the bedroom upstairs. On the first day, Rev and I drove the
truck through the city picking up treasure the frivolous rich
threw away on a whim. Our living room is full of lace and
ostrich feathers, lamb's wool rugs on the old wood floors, a
cactus in the corner sophic as a grandma.

Where's your guitar, B? Grey asks me. But they had all
belonged to Rev. A blue-green one like something under the
water and a white one that looked like a wedding cake. I did
not have a guitar of my own anymore. Never mind, she says.
Mine's out in my car, I'll be right back. I hadn't even noticed
her car out there. But sure enough, she comes back with a
beast of a guitar, dust thick as a sock under the fretboard.
She hunkers down into the sofa, says, Okay. Let's jam.

Oh, I say, leaning against the kitchen table and swirl
my mug to watch the tealeaves dance clairvoyantly. Now's
not the best time. I have so much shit to do today and it's
getting late and I...

Aw, shut up and play your guitar.

But I can't though, I tell her. I cross to the sink, abandon
my messy cup. I say, I only know some open chords, I can't
play barre chords, my timing is shit...

She sets the fucked-up guitar on the floor. And then she
stands up, grabs her bass, and walks out the door. I can see
her walking down the hill and after a few minutes I hear the
choke of her car start up and pull away. I don't even know
how she wound up in my house in the first place. I never
told her where I live.

When the house is silent again I pick up her guitar and plug it into the amp in the corner. It hums a low guttural sound like the vibration of the earth. I sit on the edge of the couch and hunch over the heavy instrument. Knowing I am fully alone and no one's eyes are on me, I am able to play. I wasn't exaggerating, my technique is garbage. But it's what I got.

I drift out into my choppy strum, hearing what it will be, the possibility of percussion and ambience in my head, and the meditation of it pulls me out of myself, into the channeled sound. My hand up and down across the sweep of strings like a ritual, a machination.

When I open my eyes, Grey is standing in front of me holding her bass. Sitting down beside me on the couch, she rests her breast in the curve of her instrument and waits for me. Play that again, she says.

We need a drummer, she says.

We're slumped at a booth in Pann's Restaurant and Grey is trying to get through a platter of French toast. The tips of her stringy hair dipping into the syrup. I push my spine into the cushion of the leatherette booth and let my eyes swim out across the red walls, the slanted ceiling rocking back and forth as if we're in an oblong boat. The honking of cars across the city pulses in time to my headache.

We were at The Jam Space all night, Grey talking shit to anyone who was standing still about our new band. Some friends she knew from the record store were playing so she schmoozed around. Nedra pulled me behind the bar and poured whiskey down my throat until neither of us could remember our reason for kissing. Rev hadn't been like that.

B, hey B. Grey snaps her fingers in front of my face.

Yeah, I answer, thinking it might be a neutral response to whatever she said.

Nice try. She throws a strawberry in my face and says, I asked you what the hell is up with you and that bartender. Because she told me she plays drums. And no offence, but I don't want to have to find another drummer if this turns out to be some temporary rebound from what's-his-name.

Yeah, I said again.

In the movies, there's always a montage that blurs over the grinding repetitive hours. This often tricks people into thinking that inspiration and success come smooth and easy, if they come at all.

For our first jam, we sit around my living room. Nedra with a three-piece kit, me with Grey's clunky guitar and Grey with her bass. I chainsmoke my voice tight and ugly. There are some blank sheets of paper in front of us. We break into a six-pack of beer to take the edge off. I can hear the kitchen clock ticking.

You're killing me B, Grey says. Improv some lyrics or a melody, anything. Let's go. She slouches on the floor with her back against the bottom of the couch, bass under her arm.

I'm not just going to break into song here, this isn't a fucking musical, I say. I got a few things we can maybe elaborate on. And we can start putting something together that I can work on when I'm alone. I crush out my cigarette into a glass ashtray and then start shredding the filter with my fingers. The smell of ash climbs up my nose.

We're here now. Let's jam. Grey gives Nedra an exasperated look.

Nedra says, You're just self-conscious and hate being put on the spot. It's making you too uptight. It takes me off-guard that I'm so easily read.

She jumps off her stool and starts dancing around the living room, singing a radio pop song. Her voice is flat and awful and she knows it and sings louder. She gets more determined with her dance moves, doing the funky chicken and some front-crawl swimming motion, plugging her nose and shaking her hips. I look over at Grey, whose eyes are narrowed in satisfaction. Then she jumps up and starts doing jumping jacks and karate kicking in my general direction.

All right, all right! I grab the guitar and the paper and start humming anything that comes to mind. Nedra and Grey fall onto the couch all out of breath.

No, there is no montage.

When we finally book a gig at The Jam Space a few months later, I feel like I'm about to face a firing squad. I remind myself of all the humans doing things far more heroic and terrifying than playing guitar songs in a dive-bar for a small crowd of disinterested drunks. But it still doesn't do anything for my nerves.

I remember something about Joni Mitchell taking a half-hour to tune her guitar onstage and how Jimi Hendrix got his gear chucked out of the tour bus window, his band leaving him behind in remote towns. If you were going to do it, you had to start.

Grey hands me a tequila shot. I lick the salt off the back of her hand. What a friend.

I remember the way I felt myself holding my breath, like at any moment I would fall from the tightrope of notes to a shameful death. Everyone seemed to be having more fun than me. People came up after and said, Great set, but it wasn't enough to calm my insides. I wanted to ask them, Really? How so? What does that mean? Am I one of those guitar players who's original and interesting even though I completely lack any skill? Because I felt like I'd opened up my mind and let everyone climb around in there and they'd left behind their cigarette butts and empty bottles and piles of trash in the corners.

I wake up in a cold sweat, a flash of harsh florescent light and I sit upright in bed, shivering in the sheets. I remember loneliness like the taste of cold metallic water. I remember tiptoeing around the edge of someone else's dream. Nedra has her arm slung across my belly in a careless intimacy. She is no fantasy.

Our second show is deep in the streets of Echo Park and it's raining.

Don't sweat it. We killed it last time, Grey assures me, swaggering toward the door of the venue.

Nedra is more sensible. The first show as a band is always like that, she says. Following it up is where it gets tricky. The second show is always the worst, it's the alchemist's law of equivalent exchange. But if we can get through tonight we'll be fine.

She grins at me. We need the shitty shows just as much as we need the successful ones. It's good for us.

You rat, you jinxed us! Grey shouts as we tear out of the place a couple hours later.

The bar owner comes running after us, shaking his huge fists. You sluts! You whore-ass bitches! If I ever see you dogs again, you'll find out what a real man will do to you!

Nedra had gotten us the gig from a bartender friend. We didn't get a sound check. Every member of the headlining band had a beard, a flannel shirt, and an identical blonde girl-friend so skinny they vanished when they turned sideways.

The audience consisted of about ten or fifteen of their college friends and two old bikers, regulars who had been there since sun up. The bikers had hard swollen guts, long beards, cracked leather pants, and faded T-shirts full of eagles and glory. Their faces were red and tough. They'd come out of the womb that way, they'd never been babies.

The crowd was unimpressed with us from the start. Nedra was wearing a T-shirt that said *DYKE*. Grey looked like an angry librarian. I hid in the bathroom until it was time to play. I didn't think the crowd would go so far as to heckle us but they did. FAGS! one of the college boys yelled when I started to sing.

Grey was already rip-roaring drunk. She screamed back, You have a micro penis!

Something went whizzing past my head and hit Nedra straight in the face. It was a big handful of olives and lemon wedges and they exploded on contact like a road kill cocktail.

What the FUCK, Grey yelled, throwing down her bass so that it squealed like a pig. But before she could do or say anything more, Nedra went sailing through the air past us and leaped on the college boy. He was so surprised he didn't even have time to scream. They fell back into the tables, pitchers of beer soaring into the air in a sweep of amber foam.

The bikers had been waiting all day for this, but they had no loyalty to anyone. One of them started punching college kids and the other grabbed Nedra around the middle where she lay on the ground swinging up at the college boy. The biker plucked her up with one arm and planted a big wet kiss on her mouth. Love me a tough chick, he roared. It was a short-lived victory. Nedra kicked him in the balls and he hit the floor hollering.

Grey tried to salvage the night and ran up to the bar. Who is the owner of this zoo? she demanded of the bartender.

That would be me! One of the bikers shouted from the floor.
Well fuck you then! And she jumped back into the fray.

Our band has been trying to land at least one gig a month. Sometimes the crowd cares, sometimes there is no crowd. But there is a buzzing around us, an electricity, and when I play I see it going out from us, our songs like birds carrying secret notes.

When we play at a bar in some up-and-coming neigh-bourhood, an agent or producer in a cheap suit offers us a big break if we can pay for it. We have a fat collection of business cards from shoddy labels and music studios nobody has ever heard of.

Grey gets into the habit of showing up at my house in the morning and we get paper cups of coffee and drive up into Mount Washington. We smoke skinny little joints and play cassette tapes, Cowboy Junkies, The Andrews Sisters. The one we play the most is a tape by Kendra Smith called *5 Ways of Disappearing*. She made the tape and then disappeared.

Grey and I, after a few months of this, find a little saloon on the side of the road called The Final Frontier. It's gener-ally empty except for a few regulars who have been sitting in the corners for over thirty years.

The Final Frontier is owned by Smith. He has white hair down to his elbows and a handlebar moustache, and when Grey sat down at the bar that first time, he started telling stories immediately. He likes to talk about the days before we were alive, when all the good stuff happened. Everyone used to come into his bar, Cher, Neil Young, The Byrds, The Doors, Carol King, Frank Zappa. And it was always summer and the front door of the place was open to the sun and the white pollen from trees blew in on the wind, covering the rough floors like snow.

Don't ask me what the world is like now, Smith says from under his heavy moustache. It's all computers and plastic. It's like a future movie that was made in the 80's when everyone was doing cocaine. We used to think that shit was funny. Now it's cold and sterile. And fucking expensive. The style and whimsy of the world has gone away. He wipes beer glasses in the gloom of the tiny bar that looks so much like a plywood lean-to built into the rock of the canyon.

Grey is with him on everything—she hates the slick gentrification that wipes the life from the city, making everything as two-dimensional as a dollar bill. She doesn't have a pocket phone. She says that if she can't touch it with her hands, she doesn't trust it. She has developed a deep love for Smith, like the love of a loyal dog. I wonder what happened to her family. I wonder what happened to mine.

Today is Sunday and we head back to the Final Frontier. We have nothing to do but sit there and listen to Smith tell us his thoughts. He closes up around five. We'd been the only ones there for the last couple of hours anyway.

You girls wanna come by for some wine? Don't worry, I'm not a creep, I don't have the energy. But it would be nice to show you the cabin, I don't got anyone to show anything to anymore.

For a minute I feel the grip of nerves, remembering that our city is over-full with freaks and rapists, but then I see Grey grabbing her coat. I trust her more than Smith or myself, so I go with her.

We get into Grey's car and follow Smith's pickup around the corner, pulling up into a long gravel driveway. There's his cabin sheltered by the trees. The interior is one room with a tiny bathroom off the side, roof beams exposed, sparse and rustic furniture. There's a big white rug on the floor and Grey and I sit on that while he pours us a wine so heavy it almost sticks to the glass. His cabin smells like raw wood, as if the logs were fitted yesterday.

Smith goes over to a record player in the corner and puts on *The End*, by The Doors. Maybe it's corny, he shrugs. But I did acid to this song when I was a kid and when I listen to it now, it comforts me. He lowers himself stiffly onto the couch, balancing his glass of wine in a rough old hand. Sometimes at night, I put it on repeat and let her play. I wouldn't mind if it was the only song in the world.

I stretch out my legs in the log cabin hidden in the woods and there we are, lizard kings and snake rides, endless rounds of blue busses and immortal mother fucks. The end.

The noise of the city shouts up at me, the performances of people, the stunts and the slang and the costumes. The money, the need. I hear the ripple of a wah-pedal and open my eyes, sun pouring over me. I'm stretched in Nedra's white sheet, the comfort of an endless morning, a bird singing the same song over again from the windowsill.

Maybe our experience can only exist on the plane of dreams, slashed through with half-asleep guitar song, collective memory thick as a rainstorm, full of wind and tears.

The truck feels like the inside of an industrial refrigerator. I've got the blues. We've been on tour for a month, driving my truck with a tiny trailer attached to the back. We stow our gear in the trailer and sleep in the truck at night. Through towns that nobody's heard of, getting paid in beer and sometimes gas fare. There's something bittersweet about these towns with their high school sweethearts and movie theatres, the repetitive days with familiar struggles.

The nights are drunk and aggressive. We put on brave faces and mount plywood stages, our lips electrocuted from cheap microphones, meeting other local bands that are sometimes kind and sometimes resentful because we are women and won't fuck them, or because we keep going and they have to stay behind.

The days are bright and painful as we ride the highway, eat fast food, read maps, call the upcoming bar from a payphone, navigate our moods.

As we head further east, the truck gets too cold to sleep in and so Grey, Nedra, and I spring for a motel. I find a ladybug crawling on my lamp before I switch it off. At night I have dreams of ladybugs, their red wings splitting as they crawl up my arms. I catch them on my fingertips and remember hearing that they're good luck, that they're an omen for love. But when Nedra curls around me, I know I am not in love. I love our band and I love our music but it doesn't get down to the depths of me.

Walls of noise, thrashing nonsensical guitar and blind rage. The tour is mouldy, cold. Nedra reveals herself to be a rowdy insomniac drunk, opinionated and cocky. There had always been booze around before, but it isn't a problem until I stay sober for one night. Nedra grabs, pushes, shoves, shouts, smashes the drums to pieces, has to stop at music stores to replace the skins. We argue over nothing. I feel like I've been air-dropped into this union and can't find the road back.

I try to write songs. I cherish rare moments alone. Music and performing become an ouroboros, dreams come in stabs that filter into the day. I hide in the motel bathroom, taking long baths. Nedra and I have drunken screaming matches in the alleys behind the bar, over what? Over nothing. And then I take refuge in the motel bathroom and she stands, inebriated, outside the door asking,

What do you want me to do? It's as far as she can come to making things right. I climb reluctantly out of the tub, open the door. I need an armistice for my own peace of mind. Maybe it's the sameness of the days that is making us crazy, being far from the city.

Grey rolls her eyes from the motel bed, goes outside for a smoke. We are losing money on the tour but we knew we would and went into it anyway, because that's what you do.

I search the faces of our small audiences and wonder what they need from us. What can I give them? What did I want every time I went and stood before a performing musician? I wanted to feel something. I want to make people feel. I don't know if I feel anything.

We come home deflated, defeated, broke. Nedra retreats to The Jam Space to pick up as many shifts as she possibly can. Grey's borrowed guitar sounds sour and twangy, it rebels under my hand, it knows it doesn't belong to me.

I didn't realize how tightly I'd been clenching my jaw until I open my mouth and it cracks. Sitting down at the kitchen table buried beneath frantic papers, empty bottles, sandy ashtrays, I start writing a letter:

Dear Rev,

I put my head down. The page sticks to my cheek like a roof shingle in a maelstrom. I don't know what else to write.

How many days have I been sitting here at the kitchen table, ink smeared along the side of my hand. The curtains closed. All of the things I love show themselves to me in absences and negative reliefs. I stand up from my chair and papers fall from my lap. The house has been submerged in the Pacific Ocean. I walk through the quiet water with wavery limbs, the colours turquoise-blue, wet cut through with light.

In my bedroom, the big white bed is empty with the sheet pulled back and the curtain moving slightly from the hot air outside, or is it a wave that moves it now.

I walk to the closet and grab a duffel bag, start putting things in at random, a jacket, some pants, a shirt. I go back down the stairs and push my feet into my sneakers. Lock the door and pocket the key. When I get into the truck, instead of heading down the road into the city, I go through the wet grey hills, pavement gleaming from headlights, tires pressing down the rain. I find Old Ranch Road.

What was this city before it was a sprawl of concrete? The roads remind me of dinosaurs and movie stars with white blossoms in their hair. The Tongva running around under the big sky, along the ridges of the canyon. I try to imagine the city being quiet because it was once.

I roll down my window and hear the wash of eternal cars. The mist beads the hair on my arms like jewelry. The Old Ranch Road is a narrow desert snake, climbing past secret houses under arches of skinny trees, winding up into the hills. I come to the turnoff into Farmers Fire Road and pull to the side, get out, and begin to walk up into the trail, the blue bowl of the earth.

The rain stops, the damp dirt crumbling under my feet. The trees look like animals, alive and waiting. I can't hear the cars anymore. Breath thumps against the wall of my chest as the trail grows steep, takes me further up the hill and away from the city, that chemical spill. The air smelling of wet dirt, green and metal.

I hear footsteps but don't turn around. My legs sing with the intensity of the foot-worn path. I keep going. The footsteps behind me keep an even, unhurried pace. I press my lips together. When I get to the guard rail I push my belly against it and look down over the edge. The messy density of the ravine. I hold my breath until my head spins. I can't hear the footsteps anymore.

Then slowly twist my head over my shoulder to the path winding down. No one is there. The landscape is empty of anything human. Except one thing.

On the edge of the trail is a pale blue guitar. The paint on its body worn down in places from sweat and hands, revealing the soft wood beneath. Opal butterflies fly up the fretboard. I scan the brush, my eyes aching from all the green, brown, grey, squinting for a detail. Whatever I think I see is gone, a blinking trick of my vision.

I stand over the instrument for a minute, waiting. The clouds come down low. I touch the guitar to feel its realness. It feels like a gentle extension of my hand. Slinging the guitar over my shoulder with its shoestring strap, it bends to my body. I head back down into the city, ready to face it again.

When I got back to the house, there was a letter waiting for me.

Dear B,

I don't know when I'll ever get back to Montreal but I want you to have this. I hope you fill the place with as much music as you can play. Make something happen. I trust you to do great things.

Love,

Sam

I shook out the envelope and the key to Anna's apartment fell into my lap.

common burn

Bands came and went, recording albums, touring Europe. I could almost touch them, but then they would dematerialize again. In the days of anxiety, there was a frantic circular toilet bowl rushing through hours that blurred and fled. I counted coins like a miser, knowing they'd slip through my fingers but never understanding how. One drunken night. Rent and groceries, what vast sums, whittled away the stash I kept hidden beneath my bathroom sink. Money was a pocketful of water. I woke up with lingering images of hungry ghosts. Counting quarters for the metro. Consulting the dwindling stash in confusion. My day job a forgettable means to an end. I showed up at the building, completed my tasks, and went back to my life again. Money seemed like a key to the secret garden, a mystery solved, heaven opened up. I didn't know the first fucking thing about it. My hands shook, my heart pounded, I raced through the hours, but there never seemed to be enough time. Why had we created limits for ourselves? The world had once been round but we'd flattened it so we could walk off the edge.

Becoming a music journalist made sense to me: I was a musician and I was too broke to go to gigs. With all of my experience hanging around bars and bands, I got picked up at one of the local publications and it almost paid my bills. The job interview was held at a bar. I told the editor "No, I've never done this before, but I'm a musician—at least I know what we're thinking, which means I won't ask them awful questions like what their favourite colour is or did they know they sound like so-and-so..." I only ever saw the editor that one time. From then on, I sent in my little columns, he published them, and that was it.

It was an easy gig, but if music journalism ever had a shred of integrity, it had been swallowed up in the proverbial town dump of music media. We were living in the future. We were tracked and chipped, sectioned off and quarantined. Broke, stifled, chemically saturated. Mostly, I felt like a flailing tornado of spastic experiences often forgotten as I ran to the next thing, full of entitlement.

In music, I'd begun to notice trends or spot certain things. I watched the rise and fall of hip kids who thought their fad jams and fashion sounds would immortalize them. I observed humble artists reluctantly coming into obscure and personal glory. The music industry was monopolized still by men who made decisions, creating lists and magazines. They formed bands, they started labels. They sang about their freedom, their power. They were convinced they were so fucking cool.

A female musician was called a Female Musician. A male musician was just a musician. With a woman you held your breath, you made a wish, you put your hopes in her. She could sell her sex at a much higher rate than men and how much pressure was put on her to do so, pedalling her private parts to whoever would pay for them in the currency of attention. To be a musician who played from the heart despite gender or commercial viability, that was special.

And something was happening inside the little groups and villages that gathered in the dark: people were whispering into each other's ears.

Was it dangerous to have someone reviewing your show? You never knew who was in your audience, witnessing the performance of a fraud or a master. Would my small perspective cause people to misunderstand, lead them astray from the intent of the song? Anyone could get on a platform and say their piece. But did it depend on how it was said? Or how the writer persuaded, pressuring young people to join a movement of pop music and specific outfits? Why did anyone have to say anything in the first place? Was that art, someone saying something and then someone else saying something back? Maybe music was inspiring enough that it compelled writers to write about it.

I went to cover an album release party on behalf of a local newspaper. The band was called Ghost Moon Wolf. They were one of those bands that had dressed themselves from the Women's Blouse Section at the Salvation Army. They wore jeans with the pant legs cut short, their tube socks pulled up, cooking oil in their hair to make it look greasy. They'd taken hours to make it look like they'd gotten dressed in minutes.

Their music was kind of nice though. They had dubbed it Blue Wave or Slacker Rock. And maybe we should have felt flattered that someone had finally validated our lives with an official genre, the way we slept until noon because we were up until sunrise doing something weird with a guitar. But something about it felt contrived.

The band was playing in someone's loft, selling beer out of the fridge in the kitchen. The doors all looked like they'd been found on the street, covered in someone's Sharpie marker wisdom. They were starting a movement of acid wash jeans and cassette tapes, flowered blouses and synthesizers, lo-fi production that sounded like it was muffled through a blanket and a cough syrup hangover.

Was I the only person who felt like a kid at Disney World, discovering the man inside the mouse costume? I hadn't even realized I'd expected something genuine until I was given something fake in its place.

I dreamed I was on tour with a band, sitting in my dressing room before the show. A soggy couch, posters curling from the walls, screaming guitar muffled through the metal door. The fluorescent lights flickered above me, turning everything a dank shade of bruise. I was sitting on a folding chair in front of a mirror trying to put on lipstick.

Outside the venue, the world had ended. The apocalypse had happened. The human species had reached its final scene. And here I was sitting in front of a mirror trying to paint my mouth red. What the hell was the matter with me?

Everything was mine but only because I was alone. All the energy I'd put into Sam, I took and siphoned into my music, like railroad tracks switching over so that the trains could go a different way. I had had no idea how much energy was actually there until I took it back and held it in my hands. It took any shape I wanted it to, so I sculpted it into songs. I sent the little tunes off into the street where they grew up motherless, became world-weary. I told myself I was a soldier. I told myself I was a deity. I told myself a lot of stuff and most of it was bullshit, but it got me out of bed.

come on home it's as it's always been

If I had a dollar for every time a song made me better, I'd have had enough cash to go into the studio myself and record all the music flying around inside me. As it was, I played in my bedroom. I played so much music in my bedroom that my songs took on the sound of a bedroom, pillow-voiced and half-dreamed up, slipping off into the vacuum of space.

Everyone else was psychedelic rock and garage surf. The west coast was sun and sand, the east coast coffee and cigarettes. The west was golden yellow and midnight blue. The east blood red and charcoal grey. I didn't know what colours I had, what sound I could claim. I listened to everyone else lay down their dreams.

Walking down the street one night, a radar blip in the black city, I heard someone say "Butterfly Jones," in a "well, well, well," tone of voice.

I whipped around and there was Tex. I had heard all about her from everyone around Montreal, as if she were bigger than the rest of us. She had a secret recording studio somewhere in the city, an underground label called Small Blue Noise. I had seen her across streets and in crowded bars but had never gotten up the nerve to approach her. When she walked around or materialized in the shadows of a concert, her dark hair pulled back into a tiny ponytail, her profile like an Egyptian god, she was always alone.

"How do you know my full name?" I asked. We were all Madonna's and Cher's to each other.

She shrugged. "I asked someone. Relax, it's not like I know your blood type."

Tex was handsome like Prince. I shouldn't have been surprised she knew my name, Tex knew everything. I'd heard many stories about her. Her mother had been a geisha in Japan. Her father was from Tunisia but had moved to Detroit to produce bands. It was said that Tex had a house in Los Angeles, that she'd been neighbours with John Frusciante. They said she'd made out with Patti Smith. I believed all of it.

I said, "Nobody calls me Butterfly, it makes me feel like I should be a fat old woman with crystals and macramé. My parents were born-again Christian hippies, probably liked the concept of metamorphosis, but I've been the same way my whole life which might be why we haven't spoken in years…" Shut up mouth, you raving lunatic.

Tex swallowed a laugh that was probably at my expense. I couldn't tell and wouldn't have blamed her. "Who has parents anymore?" she said. And then raised an eyebrow at me like she knew something about me that I didn't yet know about myself. "Where were you going with that frantic walk?"

"You ever hear of Walking Philosophy?"

She shook her head. "I'll have to do some research."

"You should." I stood there for a minute, looked over my shoulder up the street to fill the space with movement. I wasn't going anywhere.

"What do you do, besides not talk to your parents?" she asked me. A car honked. The lights turned green and red and green again.

"Not much. Play a little music…"

"As opposed to a large amount?"

"I made a demo once…I'm just a writer who can strum a guitar."

"Don't you believe in what you're doing? People scare easily. You gotta make them feel safe by showing them they can trust in you, that you're going to lead them to a good time. If you believe in what you're doing, they'll believe in what you're doing." Her hand on my arm. "You should come to my studio, it's only across the street. That way when you're playing large amounts of music you can lay down some tracks." She winked at me like a pirate.

"All right," I said, "let's go."

Tex's studio was jammed with mannequin heads and a big red velvet couch, Turkish rugs and orange amps, tambourines clattering like rays of the sun, white guitars hanging on the walls. A vast mixing board like a birds' eye view of the city at night was laid out on a plywood table. A glittering crystal chandelier dangled from the ceiling, a pirate flag fluttered above the couch. There was a wide coffee table bearing a glass bong, a bowl of black cherries, sunglasses, and a package of sour candies.

Tex clicked on a lamp, warm as an old sweater. She waved her hand around the room like performing a magic trick. "Voila. Welcome to Small Blue Noise."

"Hey, my friend Jude has that same amp," I said pointing. And then remembered he was not my friend.

"That is Jude's amp." Tex hunched over a mini fridge, clinking ice into glasses, pouring whiskey.

I sat on the edge of the velvet couch. "Why is his amp here?" My organs clenched inside me. As if his amp meant he was here in some way, shaming me.

"They're recording an album with me, what's that band? Swedish Fish? Rotten Fish? Whatever. His label actually gave them a little recording money. Shocking, I know. Then they're going on tour, they'll have their time in the sun."

"Cool," I said, pulling at a little hole in the knee of my tights until it became a big hole.

"Wanna talk about something else?" She came over and sat down beside me, handing me a glass. "What do you think of the studio?" There were reels of tape and loops of coloured wire everywhere. I pictured planes landing and operators connecting long-distance calls. "I like to touch the sound and work it out with my hands." I looked at her hands, her long and graceful fingers. "Cheers," she murmured. I touched my glass to hers, staring at the fraying holes in my clothing.

"Hey, wait a sec." Tex stopped me from bringing my glass to my mouth and touched me under my chin, raised my face so that I saw her. "You have to make eye contact when you cheers. If you don't it's bad luck." I couldn't focus my eyes, my lips already stinging from the coming whiskey. We drank and had nothing but good luck after.

"Come by the studio tonight, B. The bands are better when they have someone to play for."

I pressed the phone into my cheek, juggling a coffee cup. "When?"

"How about now? I've got this band in here and they're driving me crazy. Every member only plays keyboard. Maybe if you come by they'll start playing other instruments."

I thought about the uncharted day, my guitar at home, the open sea of the weeks. There was sun now and I had been wandering around in it. Being with Tex made everything new and since I was in a brand-new old city, I could do whatever I wanted. "I'm on my way," I told her.

Tex sat in front of the mixing board wearing sunglasses and a pale blue suit, lighting a fresh cigarette from a butt.

"Hey," she whispered in my ear. The band didn't notice me and I was glad. "When are you going to come record with me?"

"What if you don't like it?" I drummed my fingers on my knee, my foot jiggling uncontrollably. I was the captain of a leaky ship.

Tex jumped up from her chair. "Hey!" she yelled at the band. "The fuck you trying to do with that microphone?"

Outside an animal of a wind tore through the streets, lashing the windows with frozen snow. April in Montreal was sometimes spring and sometimes winter. A Buddy Holly record crackled from somewhere in my head.

Tex had arranged a night for me in her studio and I sat on a folding chair in the middle of the room. We lit a hundred candles for posterity—they filled the room with rippling light like orange water. I sipped from a bottle of white wine and Tex hit record on a big fat spool of tape.

I played five songs, the songs Jude and I had put together for my first demo, back in another time. Every song was tossing a penny into a well. Being all bound up in self-consciousness had tired me out. It took less energy to be free than it did to analyze everything to death. I closed my eyes and saw blues and greens.

Afterwards, Tex poured me a big drink and we sat on the couch, comfortable in our affection. "That was really something," she said and I could tell she was proud and surprised, like I was proud and surprised, by music and by everything else. "You sound one hundred percent like yourself."

Acknowledgements

Thank you to Ginger Pharand and Aimee Dunn for believing in this book.

Thanks to L'Escogriffe and Casa Del Popolo, among others, for being such important supporters of the Montreal music community. Thank you to Paul Brown and Ian Macpherson of the Go-Go Radio Magic Show, for being unfailing champions of Montreal's local musicians.

I would like to acknowledge the boys from the Hood-Rat Ranch. Thanks for the fodder.

Thank you to the band Palmetto for letting me write during jam sessions. Thank you to Lightbulb Alley for various situations. Thank you to the women of Kaleidoscope Horse for friendship.

I especially want to thank my family for their constant support, without which I wouldn't be anywhere good. And thank you Mark.

FLYNN

Ceilidh Michelle is a musician and author from Nova Scotia, based in Montreal. She plays music under the name Gentle Mystic. This is her first novel.